# SUDDENLY

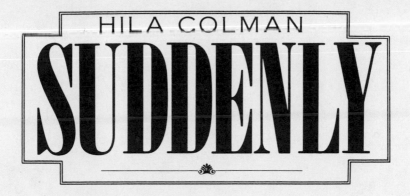

# HILA COLMAN

# SUDDENLY

WILLIAM MORROW AND CO., INC.

NEW YORK

Library of Congress Cataloging-in-Publication Data
Colman, Hila.
Suddenly.
Summary: Sixteen-year-old Emily is in the car with her
boyfriend when he hits and kills a young boy she knows,
and that death has a dramatic effect on them, the boy's
family, and Emily's own parents.
[1. Death—Fiction. 2. Traffic accidents—Fiction.
3. Family problems—Fiction] I. Title.
PZ7.C7Su 1987     [Fic]     86-28460
ISBN 0-688-05865-5

FOR JOEL

# SUDDENLY

With the blinds down and the blanket over her head, Emily Jane stuck out her hand, turned off the alarm, and snuggled back for five minutes more in bed. Getting up in the morning was the pits. Someday— that faraway, divine future day when she could do as she pleased—she would stay in bed as long as she wanted. If you're a good girl, she had always heard, get good grades, obey your parents, and avoid bad boys, you will be rewarded with a happy life: You'll marry a rich, handsome man, live in a gorgeous house, have two beautiful children, one boy and one girl, and drive a sleek black Porsche.

Emily pulled the blanket tighter over her head. Right now, having her five minutes was enough.

She'd worry about the rest of her life some other time. After all, she had all the time in the world to do it.

When she got out of bed that cool, misty, fall Halloween day, she stood in front of her window in her thin nightgown and drank in the beauty of the last of the red and orange foliage outlining the lawn. It had rained during the night and the trees had made a new scattering of leaves across the lawn. More work for Emily, but she would squeeze it in somehow. After shopping with Russ.

Russ. She liked to think about him when she was alone. Her mother said he was unreliable, always late for appointments, sometimes forgetting them entirely. Emily wasn't happy when he kept her waiting, but she didn't mind as much as her mother did—time wasn't that important to her, either. As far as she was concerned, clocks could be dispensed with. What difference did it make whether you ate lunch at twelve o'clock, one o'clock, or four in the afternoon? Going for a quick ride with her friend Becky, a dart to the shopping mall, or just lolling around could be more important.

Russ had said he was going to pick her up at ten, but if he came at ten-thirty or eleven, they'd still have plenty of time to shop. It was going to be fun buying the materials for their Halloween costumes together. She was going as Cinderella, and he as Prince Charming, but her costume was going to be more fun. Half of her was going to be in rags; her hair would be a mess, and she'd be carrying a broom. Her other half would be in a ball gown; rhinestones would dot her hair, and one foot would be clad in a silver slipper.

Emily adored Halloween. "I'm never going to be too old to go out trick-or-treating," she said. Becky had laughed at her and told her to grow up, but Emily said she would never skip going down the street to Miss Walloby's haunted house—she remembered when they were little and really thought there were ghosts—or getting some of the dark Dutch chocolate from the rich Pitkins across the way, the kind they brought home from Europe. Russ felt the same way, although some of his ideas were different from hers. He liked to take chances, he courted danger. According to him, rules were set up so that someone, preferably Russ Chassens, could test and break them.

Emily would never admit it, and last of all to Russ, but she was attracted by his spirit. Much as she argued with him not to get into mischief—and it was a sore spot in their relationship—she found him different and exciting. He wasn't accepting, the way she was.

But tonight she would have little Joey to worry about. Joey Bernstein was seven years old, and taking care of him was Emily's favorite baby-sitting job. As a matter of fact, after a couple of years of baby-sitting him, she had given up other jobs so she would be available to the Bernsteins whenever they needed her. She had promised Joey she would take him out trick-or-treating that evening, and with Joey in her care, she had a good case against Russ and his mischievous ideas.

"Grow up," Emily had told him the day before. "I'm not going to tear down mailboxes or decorate the town with rolls of toilet paper, and you're not, either. It's stupid and it's not nice."

Russ had grinned and said, "We'll see."

"Besides, I'm going to have Joey with me," Emily had pointed out, "and I'm not going to let him be part of your dumb act. I don't want you setting a bad example for him."

"We're not taking that kid around all evening," Russ had replied. "Why doesn't his brother Chet take him out? You love Joey more than you do me," he added sulkily.

"Maybe I do," Emily had told him, her eyes laughing at him. "Joey doesn't want to go with his brother, even if Chet would take him. Joey loves me. His mother promised him he could stay up until nine o'clock. Staying up late is the biggest thing in his life. We can take him trick-or-treating with us and then go to the party after we bring him home."

It was close to eleven o'clock when Russ appeared in the Simpsons' kitchen. Emily was having breakfast and chatting with her mother, a slightly plump, pretty woman. Her father had already left for his Saturday-morning round of golf. "I don't know why you kids leave it to the last day to make your costumes," Mrs. Simpson said. "It's always rush, rush with you two. When are you going to have time to make them?"

"We'll have time, don't worry. Besides, everything's reduced the last day. We can get bargains." Emily looked to Russ. "Right?"

"If you say so. But come on, let's get going."

"I've been ready and waiting for ages." Emily got up and pulled a long red sweater over her blouse and jeans. "You're the one who was late," she added sweetly.

Although it had stopped raining, the sky was dark and cloudy, and Emily held the collar of her sweater close around her neck. "What a lousy day," she said, getting into the front seat beside Russ. "I hope it clears up by tonight. I like a bright moon on Halloween night."

"No, it should be foggy and creepy like this, a good atmosphere for ghosts."

Emily snuggled up close to Russ as he backed the car out of her driveway. She had decided before he arrived that she was going to get off her mind quickly what had been bothering her. She didn't want it to bug her all day. "Russ," she began, "please promise me that you're not going to do any crazy stuff tonight."

"I never do anything crazy," he said innocently. He was driving slowly around the foggy, curved streets of the quiet, exclusive residential enclave where Emily lived. Her house was one of a group of a dozen or so houses off the main road, custom-built homes with trees and lawns whose claim to luxury was the small private lake they all shared. In the summer the man-made beach was a gathering place for the residents of the area known as Hogan's Bridge Farm. Before the houses were built, the eighty acres had been a dairy farm.

Emily's father, a successful lawyer, had bought their property because he felt it would be a safe place in which to bring up his daughter. Their neighbors were professionals, like himself, the streets were safe, the people friendly and quiet. The greatest excitement was when old Dr. Thompson took out his Model-T Ford and drove it around the block every Sunday. Emily took her secure life for granted. However, when her mother, who was not entirely comfortable in their homogenized community, worried about a smug atmosphere, Emily reassured her. "Don't worry, Mom, I know that life isn't all like this. I can survive without designer jeans, but I may as well enjoy them now." She gave her mother a teasing smile.

"It's not designer jeans I'm worried about," Vivian Simpson mumbled, but she didn't explain further.

Gazing out at the trimmed hedges and serene lawns, Emily hooted at Russ's remark. "I wish that were true, that you didn't do crazy things. Like when you and Danny set off firecrackers in the middle of the night Labor Day weekend for no reason. You're ducking the question. I'm serious. I really want a promise, no riding around with Danny and his bunch making fools of yourselves. It's just so dumb."

"Says you. You don't like Danny but I do. He's a lot of fun. You don't have to come. I'll take you home and then meet him. We have it all planned."

Russ swerved to avoid a bicycle someone had left lying on the side of the road. "I wish these kids wouldn't leave stuff in the road," he muttered.

"You're a fine one to complain." Emily was truly upset. She liked to think she had some influence over Russ. It was true that she didn't like Danny Porchak. He had dropped out of high school and hung out with an older crowd whose sole idea of fun seemed to be seeing who could consume the most beer. "Vandalism is much worse than some little kid leaving a bike in the road. You're supposed to be grown-up. I bet you'll spray stuff over shop windows too." Emily looked at him with an angry face, shaking her head despairingly. "It's so asinine. I don't believe you can really enjoy doing that stuff."

"You'd be surprised," Russ said. "It's a tradition. You just don't understand. It's our way of thumbing our nose at this snobby town—our only chance, once a year. We don't hurt anyone, but some of the people in this town need to be shaken up. They're all so smug about their expensive houses, and two-car garages, and mowed lawns. They don't care about Danny, living in a tiny, broken-down house. His father's out of work, and his mother does laundry and housework. Don't be so prissy, Emily."

"I'm not prissy," Emily yelled indignantly. "I don't see that what you're doing is any help to Danny. It just puts him all the more in the wrong, so that people say those kind of boys are no-good bums."

"I don't care what people say." Russ turned to look at Emily. "Maybe you care too much," he added. Emily was trying to decipher the expression on Russ's face. She hated to think she was being prissy, and she wanted reassurance from Russ that he was just teasing her. While Emily loved the good life, she did not want to become like some of the women in the community whose major aim was to do the "right" thing. Emily stuck to the rules because it was easier than breaking them, more out of a kind of lazy acceptance than a thought-out belief or principle.

She was trying to sort out her thoughts when suddenly the car swerved sharply and Russ jammed on the brakes. A piercing scream cut through the fog's stillness.

Emily found herself grabbing hold of Russ's arm. "He ran out, he just ran out of nowhere, I couldn't miss him." Russ was yelling wildly as he got free of her and ran out of the car. Emily followed behind him. She felt her stomach turn over and her heart thump unevenly in a peculiar way against her chest.

Russ picked up the small bundle of boy from where he lay behind the wheel and started to walk through the mist to the house opposite. Emily covered her face with her hands. Dear God! It was Joey Bernstein. She swayed dizzily for a few seconds and then ran to catch up with Russ.

They carried Joey through the back door into the

kitchen. Mrs. Bernstein turned around from the stove when she heard them, then stopped. "What happened?" She turned pale, and her eyes went from Russ, to Emily, to the bundle in Russ's arms.

"Call an ambulance, quick," Russ ordered. "Joey's been hit. I hit him, with my car." He said the words as if he didn't believe what he was saying. "He ran out, I didn't see him. . . ."

Joey was lying still in Russ's arms. His face was half covered by the grotesque mask he had been wearing, the face of a horrid, mean-looking witch. The mask looked bizarre on the small figure, clad in navy-blue corduroy overalls and a wool plaid shirt. Mrs. Bernstein held out her arms for her child.

"I think I should put him down on a couch until the ambulance comes," Russ said gently. "I don't know where he's been hurt."

"Is he breathing?" Joey's mother kept biting her lower lip, as if she were seeking relief from a physical pain of her own. Despite Russ's subtle protest, she took her boy out of his arms and held him to her. The child was moaning softly, and his mother's face brightened when he murmured, "Mommy, Mommy . . ."

After Emily had called for the ambulance, she ran to the kitchen and came back with a damp cloth to wipe off Joey's pale little face, which was smeared with tar and dirt from the road. His breathing was faint, and his mother continuously bent her head close to his head, "To see if he's alive," she explained bleakly to Emily and Russ.

Russ's mouth was twitching nervously. "He just ran out, he came out of nowhere," he kept saying. "That thick fog . . . There was nothing I could do, nothing . . ."

In a few minutes the ambulance came, and two young medics rushed into the house with a stretcher. They examined Joey briefly, and expertly transferred him to the stretcher. Mrs. Bernstein followed them outside.

"Do you want me to come with you?" Emily asked.

"I'd appreciate it . . . Joey loves you so much."

"I love him too." Emily turned to Russ and took his hand. "He's going to be all right," she said. "It wasn't your fault. Go home and I'll call you later."

Russ gave her a weak smile. "Thank you."

Emily and Mrs. Bernstein sat side by side in the emergency waiting room, close enough so that Joey's mother could take hold of Emily's hand and clutch it tightly. Mrs. Bernstein was a slim, somewhat nervous woman, her long hair wound into a bun at the nape of her neck. She was usually serious, except when she laughed and her face crinkled up with merriment. Ordinarily she laughed a lot, and Emily liked, even admired, her. Adele Bernstein had style, Emily thought. She managed to look chic in jeans as well as in the long skirts she favored, and her house had the stamp of her and her architect-husband's sophisticated personalities. Their house was always filled with the latest books and magazines, and Emily dug into them whenever she was baby-sitting and Joey had gone to sleep. The Bernsteins had moved to Hogan's Bridge Farm from New York only a few years earlier, and Emily felt that knowing them, through Joey, had brought a stylish, big-city quality to her life that growing up in Hogan's Bridge Farm hadn't given her.

"He's going to be all right," Emily comforted, wishing that she was really as sure as her words sounded.

"He will be, I know. He's had terrible falls and always been all right—and remember when he was so sick with the mumps? He bounced right back. Joey is very strong." Mrs. Bernstein's face was pale and drawn. Emily thought, She's turning old while I'm watching.

"He always plays out front," Mrs. Bernstein continued. "He never goes out on the road. He insisted on wearing that mask, he was so excited about Halloween. He was jumping around like a wild little creature this morning—so full of life. He hardly sat still to eat his breakfast—" She stopped speaking abruptly, as if the pain of her own words was too much.

They had been sitting for a short while when Mrs. Bernstein said in a calmer, almost dead voice, "I guess I should call Bob. He's at his office; he likes working there alone on Saturday when there are no interruptions."

"Do you want me to call?" Emily asked. "What about Chet? Should I call him?"

"I don't know where Chet is. You can try the house, he may be home by now. If you don't mind calling?"

"Of course not." Emily took the change given her and Mr. Bernstein's office number and went off to find a phone booth. It was a relief to be doing something. Sitting and waiting for someone to tell them how Joey was had been torture. Her mind had kept going back to those few horrible moments in the car. She hadn't seen Joey at all; he must have run out from behind the bushes the Bernsteins had close to the road. She remembered when they had planted them the spring before, to hide the house from the road. They were a pretty good size then, and Mr. Bernstein said they would get taller and thicker quickly. Firebush, he had called them, and by this fall they had grown and turned a beautiful bright red. Joey liked to play around them, but he had been cautioned dozens of times to stay on the lawn side and not to go out into the road. What in God's name had made him run out this morning? Poor Russ, Emily was thinking, he must be feeling terrible—she hoped that Mr. Bernstein would get to the hospital so that she could leave to see Russ.

Emily told Mr. Bernstein Joey had been in an accident and that they were at the hospital. He didn't ask many questions, just hung up quickly after saying he'd be right over. Then she called Chet. He told her he had just come in to get something and was about to leave again, so she was lucky to have caught him. He didn't question her either, and said he'd be at the hospital in a jiffy.

Emily didn't know Chet Bernstein very well. She had thought him a little aloof, not actually stuck-up, but outside of a few close friends, he kept to himself. She liked his looks, a dark, brooding face, but like his mother, when he laughed, his face lit up. She had the feeling that he didn't think much of Hogan's Bridge Farm, although she had never heard him say anything. He had a reputation for being a brain, and most of her friends felt that having come from New York, he thought they were a bunch of provincial hicks. Down at the beach, Chet was the one to clean up any papers or soda cans lying around, and he'd take his long swim across the lake and back by himself, rarely hanging out on the float with the rest of the kids.

Chet was a senior at Emily's high school, where

she was a sophomore, and she guessed he was probably a year and a half or two years older than her sixteen. He'd always been polite and cordial when she came to the house for Joey, but they never had had much to say to each other. Emily didn't feel comfortable with him, certain that he was far more sophisticated than she was.

It didn't take long for Chet to join his mother and Emily at the hospital. Mrs. Bernstein gave him a hard hug but left it to Emily to tell him what had happened.

Chet let out a low exclamation when she finished. "Can I go see him?"

Emily shook her head. "We haven't been able to. He's been in there for a while." She nodded toward the closed door through which Joey had been wheeled when they first arrived.

"Joey's a tough little kid," Chet said, sitting down close to his mother. "He's going to be okay." There was a strong resemblance between the mother and son, and Emily wondered about the big difference in age between seven-year-old Joey and seventeen-year-old Chet. Joey must have come as quite a surprise.

Emily wasn't sure about staying with them now. The two of them, mother and son, seemed to be in a world of their own. Not that they were talking much, but sitting close—Mrs. Bernstein with a tight hold on her son's hand—they seemed to have shut out everything except for a fierce concentration on Joey. Emily felt that she was no longer needed, but she didn't want to leave until she found out what was happening to Joey.

Emily continued to sit on the hard bench, lost in her own thoughts, which jumped from worrying about Russ to wondering what was happening behind those closed doors to sneaking an occasional glance at Mrs. Bernstein and Chet. They all stood up when a doctor came through the door. He looked at the three of them and then singled out Mrs. Bernstein.

"You are the little boy's mother?"

She nodded.

"I am sorry," the doctor said. "We did everything we could, but we couldn't save him. He never regained consciousness, so he didn't suffer. . . . I am sorry."

Mrs. Bernstein tottered and would have fallen if Chet had not held her up. She struggled to gain control of herself. "You mean . . . ?"

The doctor nodded his head. "I am sorry," he repeated.

Chet led his mother to a chair and brought her a glass of water. The doctor stood by. "If you would like a sedative?"

"No, no thank you." Mrs. Bernstein's face was drained of color. She sat in the chair looking as if she might never move.

Emily felt dizzy. She hoped that she wasn't going to faint. Suddenly the hospital seemed overpoweringly hot, and she wasn't sure she could continue to breathe. Somehow she got herself over to the window and rested her forehead against the cool glass. She looked outside the window and down below where some children were playing, little kids wearing Halloween masks and running around the backyard of a house. Then she felt the welcome relief of tears pouring down her cheeks.

Emily turned back to Mrs. Bernstein, knelt on the floor beside her, and buried her face in her lap. She must have served as a release for the older woman, who put her arms around Emily and let her own tears flow. The two of them held each other close.

They were all still in the waiting room when Mr. Bernstein appeared. He didn't have to be told anything; seeing them was enough. He sat down next to his wife and folded her into his arms.

Chet stood to one side of his parents, staring out at the room with a bleak expression on his face. Emily got up to leave. She felt that the family needed to be alone. She said good-bye softly and turned to go, but Chet held her back with a gesture.

"Tell Russ to stay out of my way. I don't know what happened, and it's not really important anymore. But I don't want to see the guy who killed my brother, understand?"

Emily nodded meekly. There was nothing she could say. It was Mrs. Bernstein who lifted her head from her husband's shoulder and looked at her son. "Chet, darling, don't speak that way. We have enough . . . we don't need any more right now. I'm sure it was an accident. It wasn't anyone's fault—"

"We'll have to see about that," her husband replied gruffly. "The police will investigate if anyone is to blame. I know how you feel, son," he added, wiping the tears from his face.

The cool air felt good to Emily after the stuffiness and medicinal smell of the hospital. She walked for a few blocks, undecided where to go. She didn't know whether to go to her own house or to Russ's, and she hadn't given a thought as to how she was going to get to either place. It was a long walk to both. Without wanting to think about anything, she simply kept walking. Everything had happened so quickly that morning—it seemed that when she had gotten out of bed and thought about her Halloween costume, it had to have happened in another century. She couldn't believe she was still the same person whose major preoccupation had been to keep Russ out of mischief. Mischief. Nothing he could have done— not tons of rolls of toilet paper, nor dozens of cans of shaving cream—could match what had happened that morning. She didn't want to think about Russ. Thinking about him forced her to think about herself. Were they both guilty of killing Joey?

The thought was too horrible to contemplate. Emily kept going over in her mind the few minutes in the car before she heard that unforgettable scream. She and Russ had been arguing. His voice had been annoyed, and she had been angry. If they had not been talking, if they had been paying attention to the road, would they have seen Joey in time? Had Russ been looking at her instead of at the road? Oh, God, why couldn't she have waited to argue with him until after they'd gotten to the shopping mall? Why did she have to start up in the car? The awful questions kept spinning round and round in her head until Emily felt that if they didn't stop, her head would burst open from the pressure mounting up.

The trouble with this town, Emily thought as she walked, was that you couldn't get from one place to another without a car. There were no buses, no trains. Lots of cars passed her, but Emily didn't feel like trying to hitch a ride. The idea of getting into a car was repulsive. So she kept on walking.

Eventually she got to Russ's house. The door was open, and she found him sitting by himself in front of the television set. It wasn't turned on; he was just sitting staring at the blank glass.

"I thought you'd come to the hospital," Emily said by way of greeting.

"I didn't feel like driving," Russ replied in a low, flat voice. He looked up and met her eyes. "How is he? Is he okay?"

Emily shook her head. "He isn't. Oh, Russ—" She broke down into sobs and fell into a chair, exhausted. "He died," she managed to say. "My darling little Joey . . . I can't believe it, I just can't."

Her face was buried in her arms, and when she finally looked up, Russ was pacing around the room, his face white and tense.

"I knew he was going to die," Russ said dully. "I knew it when I picked him up in my arms. I don't want to talk about it, Emily. There is nothing to say."

"Russ, I have to talk about it, I just do. Did we kill him? Tell me what you really think. Was it our fault?"

"There's no *we* about it. *I* was driving. You didn't

do anything. Emily, I didn't see him, I just didn't see him. He came out of nowhere. Out of that darned fog. He ran into the car. God, I've been doing nothing but thinking about it. It was that stupid mask. I think it was on so that his eyes were covered. He just ran, he didn't see anything. I don't think he even knew he was on the road. He ran into the car." Russ was running his hand through his hair, and his eyes were searching Emily's face.

"But if we hadn't been arguing," Emily said feebly. "If I hadn't distracted you—"

"You didn't do anything," Russ said fiercely. "Don't give yourself a guilt trip. We're not guilty." He was yelling now. "You understand, we're *not guilty.*"

Emily had no answer for him. His vehemence frightened her. She realized that they were both in shock, but she had the feeling that Russ was also frightened. Suddenly she remembered the police. She hadn't thought about what they might do. There would certainly be an investigation. Would they accuse Russ of murder? Of manslaughter? She couldn't let him face that alone. Even though he was the one driving, she was as guilty as he. *She had taken his attention away from the road.*

They both jumped when the phone rang. Russ let it ring, but it was so insistent, he went to the hall to answer it. Emily heard him speak for a few minutes, but she couldn't make out what he was saying. When he came back into the family room where they had been talking, he had a sad smile on his face. "That was Jimmy wanting to know when you and I were going to the party tonight," Russ said.

"Did you tell him what happened?"

"No, I didn't. I couldn't. He'll hear about it soon enough."

The party. Emily had her arms crossed around her body, holding herself close, as if to keep from shivering. The early morning, thoughts of Halloween, costumes, trick-or-treating, the party . . . it all seemed to have happened in another life. She had woken up that morning a happy girl. Her biggest problem had been to buy and make her Cinderella costume. She was never going to be that same innocent, carefree girl again. A few minutes in a car had changed her life. She didn't know how it was changed—there was no way of knowing—yet she was certain that a change had taken place. From now on there would be no morning when she woke up that she could be certain that the day would end as it began—anything could happen, nothing would be predictable, assured. The thought gave her an odd feeling, as if for the first time she was seeing life as it really was, a series of happen-sos, of accidental events. She had thought that people had control of their lives, that they could arrange events and make free choices, but now she was convinced that was not so.

She felt overwhelmed by her own sense of helplessness. What was the use of doing anything, she wondered bleakly, if suddenly, in a matter of minutes, a young life like Joey's could be snuffed out for no reason?

News travels fast in a small town, and by the time she walked home from Russ's house, Emily discovered that her mother had already heard of the accident. Apparently Mrs. Simpson had been hovering at the door, because she grabbed Emily into her arms as soon as she came in. "Are you all right? Did you get hurt?"

"No, I'm okay. You heard what happened?"

"Mrs. Anderson called and said there'd been an accident with Russ's car and that little Joey was hurt. I've been frantic. She didn't know about you, and I didn't know if you were in the car. I couldn't decide whether to go out to look for you or just to wait here.

I called the Bernstein house, but there was no answer."

"No, there wouldn't be, they're all at the hospital. Oh, Mom . . ." Emily turned to her mother and burst into sobs. "Mom . . . Joey's dead, we killed him . . . I don't know how it happened, I'll never know."

Her mother held her close and didn't let go until Emily stopped her heavy sobbing. She led her to a sofa and sat down beside her. "Now tell me what happened. Tell me everything."

Emily told her mother about the events leading up to the accident, and her argument with Russ. She started to cry again but gained control of herself when she had to talk about Joey. "I didn't see him. Russ didn't see him. Suddenly we heard this horrible scream, and Joey was under the car. . . . I'll never forget that sound, not as long as I live. It was awful . . ."

Her mother put her arms around her and held her against her breast. "My poor darling, what a terrible thing. . . ." Mrs. Simpson lifted Emily's face so that she could look at her. "But it wasn't your fault, darling. I doubt it was even Russ's fault. Things like this happen. Cars are treacherous. I hate them. I wish we still rode around in carriages with horses."

Emily gave her mother a weak smile. "I know. You hate most modern inventions except Scotch tape." She gave a deep sigh. "I'll never get over this. My life will never be the same. And I *do* feel guilty. If I hadn't been arguing with Russ . . ."

"You mustn't think that way. You're only hurting yourself. Maybe your life won't be the same, but maybe you won't take everything for granted." She waved her hand to the pretty room they were sitting in with its fine antique tables and chintz-covered sofas. "We live in such a comfortable, safe world that when something like this happens, it's a big shock."

"It's awful," Emily agreed. Talking to her mother made her feel a little better. Her mother gave her the feeling that life had to go on, and that from somewhere Emily would find the strength to deal with it.

Emily knew the police officer who came to see her later that day. His son had graduated from her school the year before. Sitting on the sofa beside her mother, she told her story again. "What about Russ?" she asked when she was finished. "Is he going to be in trouble?"

"I don't think so," the officer told her. "He wasn't drinking, he was driving slowly, he took the lie detector test, and that was okay. I guess it will depend on the Bernsteins, whether they bring charges. So far it looks like one of those tragic accidents. The kid ran out into the road and the car. We examined the tire marks, there wasn't much Russ could do. It's hard on him. He's a victim too."

"I know," Emily said, thinking that she was also a victim. "But not like Joey," she added. "Russ is alive. He and I both are."

Sitting alone in her room later that evening, Emily could hear the sounds of laughter outside, cars going by, and the occasional blare of a car radio. She wished she could shut out the noise; it seemed blasphemous to her that all this gaiety should be taking place when only that morning . . . She couldn't believe that funny, adorable Joey was not going to laugh anymore. For a kid that age he'd had an incredible, quick sense of humor. Only two days before when she had put one of her rock records on his record player, he had turned it off, saying in a very grown-up way that her music was boring.

"Why is it boring?" she had asked.

"Why is the sky blue?" he'd shot back.

"I don't know."

"Then don't ask me dumb questions," he'd said with his impish grin.

She wished she could stop thinking about Joey. Emily got up from her bed and went downstairs. Her parents were in the living room talking quietly. "Do you think I should go over to the Bernsteins'?" Emily asked nervously.

"I don't think so. Not tonight," her mother said. "I imagine they want to be alone. You can go soon, though, and I'll come with you."

Emily felt relieved. She dreaded seeing Joey's parents, but at the same time she felt a pull toward them, a need to be included in their mourning. Mrs. Bernstein had often said, "You're like one of the family, Emily," and now she yearned uneasily for an affirmation of that acceptance.

She sat listening to her parents talk about a legal case her father was working on without actually hearing what they were saying. Her mind was far away when there was a knock on the front door. Mrs. Simpson went to open it, and when she returned, Russ's parents were with her. They were both tall, large people, exuding health and vigor. Sandy Chassens was the best woman tennis player at the local country club, and her husband was proud of a couple of silver cups he had won in golf tournaments. Although neither one was fat, they seemed to fill a room when they were in it together.

"Where's Russ?" Emily asked after the greetings and drinks or coffee had been offered and declined.

"He's out with Danny. Russ didn't want to stay home tonight." Mrs. Chassens threw her cape across the back of a chair and sat down.

Emily was shocked. "Out tonight? How could he go out tonight, and with Danny!"

"Why not Danny? Danny's a good friend of his. I urged him to go. I don't want Russ to mope around the house thinking he's committed a crime. The accident wasn't Russ's fault." His mother said the last sentence as if every word were underlined.

"There's nothing Russ can do about it," Mr. Chassens added. "It's a terrible tragedy, but what's done is done."

Emily felt stunned. She couldn't stand the pat phrases, the calm acceptance of the tragedy.

"And what have you got against Danny Porchak?" Russ's father changed the subject abruptly. "Because he doesn't live in a nice house? We didn't bring up Russ to be a snob."

"I'm not a snob, either," Emily said indignantly, stung by the accusation. "I don't care about Danny's house, I just don't like him. I don't like what he does. Being poor doesn't make him great."

Seeing Emily so uncharacteristically adamant, her father asked, "I don't know Danny, but why don't you like him?"

"He just hangs around. If he's so poor, why

doesn't he get himself a job, or at least finish high school? I wish I knew what he lives on. I think he's a bad influence on Russ."

"Don't worry about Russ, he can take care of himself," Mr. Chassens replied confidently.

Emily wanted to say, "You don't know anything. You don't know what you're talking about or what Danny really is." But she was in no mood for arguing and kept quiet. Why were they talking about Danny, anyway? Who cared about Danny now? Russ's parents didn't want to think about Russ and Joey, that was what it was all about. She wanted to get up and leave, but she didn't feel like being up in her room alone, either. "I can't believe Russ went out partying tonight," she murmured.

"I don't know if he's partying," Mrs. Chassens said sharply. "But he's not staying home moping. You should go out, too, Emily. You're not going to do anybody any good by making this a worse tragedy than it is. For you and Russ to torture yourselves will help no one."

"I'm not torturing myself, but I have *feelings*. I couldn't possibly go out and enjoy myself tonight, Mrs. Chassens. It would make me feel terrible. I loved Joey—I've known him since he was a baby. I've spent hours and hours, days and days with him. He wasn't just an ordinary kid to me."

"Yes, I know," Mrs. Chassens said, as if she were trying to be sympathetic.

Emily soon excused herself and went back to her room. She was restless and unhappy, resenting the Chassens' flip answers and the fact that life was going on as usual. She felt that everything should stop, that at least there should be a period of mourning.

Joey's funeral was a private family service, and as much as Emily longed to make some contact with the Bernsteins, she didn't dare put in an appearance at their home afterward. Her mother was afraid that seeing Emily would only upset Mrs. Bernstein more.

The day after the funeral the local newspaper came out with an editorial that divided the community and infuriated Emily. It was headlined A SENSE-LESS KILLING—WHO WAS TO BLAME? While the editorial made some small attempt to chastise both parents and teenagers, it pointed the finger at the teenagers for being uncaring and wrapped up in themselves, and for riding around uselessly in their cars. Without saying so outright, it virtually blamed Emily and Russ for Joey's death.

Emily wept when she read it. "It's unfair. The police aren't blaming us, I don't think the Bernsteins are—how dare this paper make a judgment?"

"Newspaper editorials do it all the time," her father said. "They like to stir up controversy. It makes
more people buy the paper."

"It's mean. Can't we do anything about it? Sue
them for libel?" Still teary-eyed, Emily was very
angry.

"I'm afraid not. They didn't mention your name,
nor really accuse you directly. I'd say forget about
it." Mr. Simpson gave his daughter a sympathetic
but brief hug. Emily wished that her father didn't always look busy even when he wasn't. Although she
had to admit that most of the time he was working
on something—a new brief, his accounts and taxes,
bills for the house, or reading a law journal—she
couldn't remember ever seeing him just sitting down
and doing nothing.

"Do you think it's wrong for teenagers to ride
around, to just hang out without really doing something?" Emily asked.

They were sitting in her father's study, and he
leaned back in his swivel chair and eyed her
thoughtfully. "I'm not sure. I think there is some
truth in the editorial—that a lot of teenagers are too
self-involved and are thoughtless, but I think it's
wrong to generalize. I don't think it's wrong for kids
to just hang out, as you say, if that's not all that they
do. If they're busy with schoolwork, and sports, and

helping at home, or have jobs, then if they want to do nothing with the time that's left, they're entitled. If they have any time left," he added with a grin.

"Fat chance," Emily said.

On the Saturday after Joey's funeral, Emily and her mother had decided it was time for them to go see the Bernsteins.

Emily was nervous about the visit.

She knew that the Bernsteins sat Shiva, the Jewish mourning period when the immediate relatives stayed at home for seven days after a death in the family. Emily didn't know what to expect, and she wasn't sure how the Bernsteins would receive her.

She stood with her mother outside their house, almost deciding not to go in at all. "You're going to have to face them eventually," Mrs. Simpson said. "I think they'll appreciate your coming. They know how you felt about Joey. Come on, Emily."

"But maybe they hate me now."

"I doubt it. Besides, you can't keep on carrying this guilt. I think it's important for you to see them."

The door was open, apparently for visitors, and Emily and her mother went in. The three Bernsteins were there—Joey's parents and his brother Chet, and an older woman and two men who turned out to be

Mrs. Bernstein's mother and her two brothers. They were all sitting in the Bernsteins' sunny living room. Emily didn't know what she had expected, but she was relieved that they were sitting and quietly chatting.

Chet stood up and came forward while Emily and her mother stood at the doorway. His face was pale and tense. He was obviously upset at seeing them.

"We came to pay our respects," Mrs. Simpson said simply, before Chet could speak. "We are all so terribly sorry."

"Thank you," Chet said coldly. "But I think you had better go."

Emily turned away and tugged at her mother. "Come on, I knew we shouldn't have come. I'm sorry," she said to Chet.

But Mrs. Bernstein had come over to them and had her hand on her son's shoulder. "Please, Chet. This is no time to hurt people. I'm glad Emily came, she had to." She put out her hand to Emily and led her into the room. Emily took one look at the older woman's tired face and burst into tears. "I'm so sorry," she mumbled. "I don't want to bother you. . . ."

"You're not bothering me," Mrs. Bernstein said. "You help me feel close to Joey." After introducing the Simpsons to her relatives, Mrs. Bernstein began to talk about Joey. "He adored Emily," she told the others. "We never had a problem going out when he knew Emily was coming to stay with him. I don't know what those two talked about, but when we were home, we could hear them chatting away and giggling as if they were two kids the same age."

Mrs. Bernstein, usually a rather quiet woman, went on talking as if she couldn't stop, and she held on to Emily's hand as if, had she let go, she might collapse.

All the time that his mother talked, Chet sat stony-faced, avoiding Emily's eyes, and looking as if he couldn't wait for her and her mother to leave. Finally he stood up and said, "Mom, I think it's time for you to take one of your tranquilizers."

"Yes," his father agreed. He had hardly spoken a word but had watched his wife with an anxious face. "I think perhaps you'd better go." He nodded to Emily and Mrs. Simpson. "Thank you for coming," he added coolly.

Chet walked them to the door. "Please don't come back," he said. "She's wound up enough, and seeing Emily doesn't help. It doesn't help any of us."

"I'm sorry," Emily mumbled.

As they walked home, Emily said to her mother, "I knew we shouldn't have gone. It was awful."

"I don't think so," Mrs. Simpson replied. "I think it was good for that woman to talk about her son. Why shouldn't she? She was glad you came. Her husband and Chet don't know everything."

"I'll never go there again," Emily said firmly.

Just one week after Joey's death, Emily, for the first time in her life, thought seriously about dropping out of school. The week started out miserably.

Monday morning, the principal of the high school, Mr. Carey, a serious, socially conscious young man, decided to have the entire school participate in discussions about Joey's death and the paper's editorial: Were teenagers guilty of what the paper accused them?

Emily loathed the thought of these discussions and dreaded participating in them. In her social studies class, where her class had its talks, she was soon the center of all eyes. She felt self-conscious and embarrassed and hated the questions that were thrown at her. While their teacher tried her best to keep the discussion away from Emily and Russ, the talk kept getting bogged down in speculations on what had really happened that tragic Halloween day.

Emily burst into tears and had to leave the room when Chet stood up and said in his quiet, deep voice, "It's wrong to try to condemn all teenagers for what happened. Because two nitwits were too involved with their own stupid conversation to pay attention to the road is no reason to blame all teenagers."

The class applauded him, and only Becky Haynes ran out after Emily to see if she was all right. Emily was in the girls' lavatory weeping, and Becky took her in her arms. If Emily had a best friend, it was Becky, a large, warm girl whom Emily teased as being a born mother.

"Don't pay any attention to what they're saying. Chet knows better, I'm sure he doesn't mean what he said. He's just hurt and mad and has to let it out on someone." Becky gave Emily a tissue to wipe her face. "It wasn't anybody's fault. Even the police said that."

"I know, but no one believes it." Emily was trying to hold back her sobs. "I'm going to stay home, I can't come to this school anymore. Everyone hates me and Russ."

"Don't say that. I don't hate you. Lots of kids

don't. It's that stupid piece in the paper that's got everyone stirred up. They never should have printed it."

"But they did. And maybe they're right. Maybe if I hadn't been arguing with Russ . . . but he wasn't looking at me, he had his eyes on the road. Oh, God, I don't really know how it happened!"

"It was one of those things. Come on, let's go back to class. Just look them in the eye and don't let anyone bother you." Becky tugged at Emily's arm. "Come on."

"Easier said than done, but I'll try."

Emily did go back to the classroom, but instead of "looking them in the eye," she tried to avoid anyone's eyes. She sat at her desk and kept her eyes glued to a book she held in front of her.

Getting through the rest of the day was torture, and when the last bell rang, she made a dash to get out without talking to anyone. But she wasn't fast enough. In the hall she ran into Russ. She had been trying to avoid him since the accident. Somehow hanging out with him now made her feel uncomfortable, as if they were two criminals sticking to each other.

Besides, she didn't understand the way he was reacting to the accident, and she didn't like it. On the surface Russ was behaving with a bravado Emily found phony: He went around saying that yes, it was a terrible tragedy, but thank God he wasn't at fault, he couldn't live with it if he had been to blame. It seemed to Emily he was going overboard trying to convince everyone and himself that he was blameless. But at the same time he was hanging out more and more with Danny Porchak, drinking too much beer, and talking too much about the accident. "If he's sure he's so innocent," Emily had said to Becky, "why does he keep talking about it and drinking so much? I think deep down he doesn't believe a word of what he's saying. I'm worried about Russ, I think he's in real trouble."

"I agree. Maybe you should talk to him," Becky had suggested. "I think he's keeping a lot inside and needs to talk it out."

"I'm no psychiatrist. I don't feel like talking to him. I don't even feel like seeing him anymore. Maybe I'm being selfish," Emily said, "but I don't feel comfortable with Russ now. He has to work this out himself, in his own way, and so do I. We're no good for each other right now."

Even as Emily spoke, she had a twinge of conscience about Russ. Her conscience told her that this was no time to dump him; however, she justified her desire not to see so much of him with the fact that he wasn't going out of his way to see her, either. He seemed to be avoiding her, too, and she surmised that unlike her, he wanted to forget about Joey. Also, he knew that she didn't like Danny, and that was someone Russ was spending a lot of his time with now.

Now he greeted her with a friendly, casual smile. "How're you doing?"

"I'm okay. What about you?"

"I'm fine. Why shouldn't I be?"

"No reason. I'm glad you're fine." She laughed with him. "Now that that's out of the way, how are you really?"

"I really am okay. What about you?"

"I'm furious about that dumb editorial in the paper. Are the kids giving you a hard time?"

"If they are, I'm not paying attention. I don't care about the paper, and I don't care what anybody says or wants to think. You and I know what happened, and the police know, and that's all that matters. Forget it, Emily, it's over. Past history."

"I wish I could. But I can't. I miss Joey, I miss going over to the Bernsteins'. It's different for me."

"You're making it different. We're going over to Reuben's tonight, you want to come?" Reuben's was a hangout for the high-school crowd. There was beer for those old enough to drink it, there was live music on weekends, and during the week there was the jukebox.

"You going with Danny?" Emily asked.

"Yes." Russ gave her a look that said, "So what?"

"Thank you. No." She turned to pass him in the hall when she bumped straight into Chet Bernstein walking hurriedly in the opposite direction. Emily didn't realize they had hit each other that hard, but the books Chet was carrying fell out of his arm onto the floor. Emily stooped to help pick them up.

"Don't bother," Chet said coldly. "I can handle it. Why don't you look where you're going? Or," he added, glancing at Russ, "don't you and your boyfriend ever look in front of you?"

"That's a dirty crack," Russ said. "We were just standing here. You're the one who knocked into Emily. Maybe you should look where *you're* going."

Chet had gathered his books together and faced Russ. "I've been itching to punch you out, but so far I've managed to control myself. It hasn't been easy, I can tell you, and I may not hold out much longer. I'm warning you. Just stay out of my way and don't bug me."

"Are you trying to scare me? Listen, buddy, any-time you want to fight, I'm ready. As far as I'm concerned, this is as good a time as any. You want to come outside, you can have your chance at punching."

The two boys stood facing one another, holding each other's eyes coldly. "Come on, you two," Emily said. "What's the sense of fighting? It's stupid and proves nothing. Come on, Russ, let's go."

"No," Chet said. "I've had enough. Come on, let's go outside."

In spite of Emily's pleas, Russ led the way to the yard in back of the school with Chet close behind him. A distraught Emily followed. The boys took off their outer jackets, dropped them on the ground, and faced each other. There had been a frost that morning, and while the sun had shone at noon, now, in mid-afternoon, the sky was cloudy and the air felt raw and cold. Looking up at the gray sky, Emily pulled her parka close around her and thought there might be snow by evening. She wished frantically that there was some way to stop the fight.

But there was no one around to help. She could hear the last bell and knew that everyone would be making a dash for their buses, lined up in front of the building. The back, where they were, was deserted.

The boys didn't waste any time. After a few minutes of sparring, they were locked in a struggle that had them both on the ground. First it was Russ pounding away at Chet, and then Chet turned him over and was in control. When Chet stopped for a breath, Russ staggered to his feet, pulled the other boy up with him, and started pummeling him all over again. They went on that way, first one winning, then the other, until their own exhaustion had them both sitting on the ground.

They sat, staring at each other for a few minutes. Chet was the first to get up. He brushed himself off and picked up his jacket. "Stay out of my way, boy," he said, "or you'll get worse next time."

"This isn't the end," Russ threatened, pulling himself up. "Next time I'll finish you off." Chet gave him a cold stare and turned to go.

"So what did you prove?" Emily cried out angrily. "You're both ridiculous. I don't think Joey would think much of either one of you," she added tartly. "Good-bye, I'm going home." She turned abruptly and walked away. Neither of the boys attempted to follow her.

Emily had missed her bus but she didn't care. It was a long way to get home, but she was so filled with pent-up emotions, she welcomed the exercise. Much as she had wanted to stop the boys from fighting, she was envious of their ability to have that outlet. She, too, felt like punching someone or something hard. Not Russ or Chet—just something. Over and over again in her mind she lived those few minutes before she heard Joey's scream. Had she distracted Russ? If she had kept quiet, would Russ have seen Joey and been able to stop in time? The questions kept tormenting her. Deliberately she tried to focus on the larger questions they had been discussing in school: Were she and all her friends, her whole generation, an uncaring, self-centered, superficial bunch, greedy for amusement, for more VCRs, more cars, more clothes, more material wealth?

Emily had never given much thought to herself in relation to the rest of the world—she knew there was poverty, she sometimes worried about a nuclear war, but her own role in the scheme of things had not occurred to her. Was feeling safe so important? Did she want to be like the people in Hogan's Bridge Farm, whose happiness seemed to depend on how often they could buy a new car? She wanted to be a good person—she wanted to get good grades, to go on to college, and to have a career. Someday she wanted to get married and have a family. But what she meant by a "good" person she couldn't say. She knew more what she didn't want: She didn't want to get mixed up with dope or alcohol, or be mean, or not have friends, or have fights with her parents. The sense-lessness of Joey's death seemed to be serving as a microscope focused into her brain—or her soul, she didn't know which—and holding everything up to the light to be examined. What she would see in that microscope, Emily wasn't yet sure.

She had been walking, oblivious of the streets she was passing. She walked through a working-class residential section with both sides of the street lined with small, trim, boxlike houses, then the familiar Caldor shopping mall. When she passed the mall, she had a stretch of open highway to cover before she came to the more exclusive section where she lived.

Emily was walking against the traffic, hugging the shoulder of the road, when a car stopped on the other side, headed in her direction. Chet stuck his head out. "You want a ride home?" he called to her.

Emily was surprised. But she was tired, and grate-fully she crossed the road and got in beside him. "Thanks very much." She glanced over at him. "Are you okay? Your lip's swollen."

"Yes, I know." He kept his eyes straight ahead, and his narrow, sensitive face was stern. Emily liked Chet's face. He looked like a scholar—deep-set dark eyes; a prominent, strong nose; but with a soft mouth that said, "I'm not always as serious and stern as you think." A lot of the girls, including Becky, found Chet attractive.

"What made you stop for me?" Emily asked with a sidelong glance. "I know you hate me."

"Don't flatter yourself," he said curtly. "I don't feel anything as strong as hate." Then, in a kinder voice, "It's a long walk home. I'm going the same way, so what?" He kept his eyes ahead but he gave a small smile. "My mother taught me good manners."

"How is your mother?" Emily asked.

"Not good. As a matter of fact, she's terrible. It's awful for her, she adored Joey."

"I know."

He gave her a swift glance. "I suppose you do know." He stopped the car for a red light and then looked at her as if seeing her for the first time. "I guess it hasn't been easy for you, either, has it?"

"No, it hasn't," she said quietly.

They didn't speak again until Chet pulled up in front of Emily's house. Then, gathering her courage, she thanked him for the ride and said, "Do you think your mother would like me to come see her? I know you asked me not to come back, but I think about her a lot."

He stared at her blankly, as if the question didn't quite register. "I don't know what my mother would like. She keeps pretty much to herself."

Chet drove away and left her watching the car go down the street and around the corner toward his house. Emily was thinking of the expression on his face, trying to find an answer to her last question in it. But she couldn't figure out if he had only been surprised, or if he thought it a good or a bad idea for her to visit Mrs. Bernstein. She'd have to decide for herself. Emily turned and went into the house, exhausted. It had been a long, emotion-filled day.

Russ, Emily learned, did not get over the fight with Chet easily. She had been more or less avoiding him, but Becky reported that Russ was going around saying he was "going to get Chet Bernstein." As Becky explained, "Russ claims that Chet is smearing him, claiming that he killed his brother, and he, Russ, is going to shut him up once and for all."

The girls were at Becky's house, sitting in the attic bedroom Becky had turned into her own haven of books, posters, clothes draped over chairs, musical instruments, and odds and ends, including a three-foot-high tin that had once contained pretzels and was now a catchall for anything from tennis balls to headbands.

"I don't think that's true," Emily said. "Chet wouldn't say that. He thinks that maybe Russ isn't entirely blameless—" She broke off, and her eyes filled with tears. "Everything's awful. I don't know what I think myself anymore. Oh, God, if I could only turn the clock back."

"I'm afraid you can't," Becky said in her easy, practical way. "I think you should see Russ. He's going to get into serious trouble one of these days with his drinking and all."

"What can I do for him?" Emily dried her eyes and picked up Becky's brush to brush her hair.

"You'd be a good influence. You're a friend of his, and he needs his friends now."

"He's got his friend Danny."

"You don't think much of Danny, and I don't really know him. I think you should call up Russ and make a date with him."

"I don't know if he even wants to see me." Emily knew she was reaching for excuses.

"Why wouldn't he? Russ was crazy about you."

"*Was.* But maybe not now. If I did call him, would you come out with us? I don't want to be alone with him and just talk about the accident. Or listen to him shoot his mouth off about Chet."

"Yes, sure. What would we do?"

"I don't know, it's your idea." Emily brushed her

hair vigorously and returned the brush to Becky's bureau. "I don't want to go to Reuben's, Russ's favorite hangout these days. Maybe we could go across to the Valley Pub. It's farther, but I hear it's fantastic. We could go on a Friday night when they have music."

"Super," Becky agreed. "I'll ask Hank if he wants to go. He always has money."

"You sound mercenary," Emily said with a grin.

"I don't mind paying my way, but if a guy has money, so much the better."

When Emily left to go home, the girls promised to call the boys and get back to each other that evening.

Emily put off calling Russ until after dinner. She had been spending more time than usual at home since the accident, and both of her parents had made a point of spending time with her. They had gotten into the habit of sitting around the dinner table talking, long after they were finished eating. Emily's father wanted her to forget about the accident and amused his wife and Emily with stories about the cases he was handling. Emily knew he was trying to keep her from being depressed and she appreciated it, but she was more comfortable when she was alone with her mother and could talk about Joey and her own confused feelings.

Emily felt that all her feelings and attitudes were being put under scrutiny these days. She was questioning everything. She adored her father—an attractive, successful man, who always put her friends at ease when they came over. Becky had once confessed that when she got married, she hoped she'd marry someone like Emily's father. But now, for the first time, Emily was becoming aware of her mother's less than total satisfaction with the life they were leading.

As Emily was learning, Vivian Simpson had never become completely at ease in the middle-class comforts of Hogan's Bridge Farm. She had grown up on a tobacco farm along the Connecticut River, and although her widowed mother had sold off most of the acreage and Hogan's Bridge Farm wasn't that far away, her marriage to Steve Simpson had taken her into another world. He had been a young lawyer then, fresh out of law school; but he was bright and ambitious, and it didn't take him long to become a partner in a successful law firm with offices in the nearby town of Sudonberry. For Vivian Simpson that meant being a hostess to his clients—some of them high-up corporate executives with ultra-fashionable wives whose designer clothes and weekend trips to Paris intimidated her.

Although Mrs. Simpson was not a misfit, nor a

complainer, every now and then she let slip a line that was a clue to feelings of insecurity and aloofness. And in some things she was quite adamant. She flatly refused to join the local country club even though her husband kept saying he liked the golf course and that many of his clients belonged.

In her talks with her mother Emily freely admitted that she was shaken up by the article in the paper. "Do you think what they said is true?" she asked. "That teenagers just care about themselves?"

"No, I don't," her mother said. "I think you kids have a hard time because it is easy to satisfy your whims. Here in Hogan's Bridge Farm we are living in an affluent society—it's not like a big city. We don't see run-down houses and people living on the streets. You can be sure there aren't any families in Hogan's Bridge Farm on welfare. You can't blame teenagers if they only think of themselves and of having a good time. The whole community is sheltered from any outside influence, from anything that might spoil their complacency. Nobody goes near those few broken-down houses near the closed-down factory. I worry about your growing up in this rarefied atmosphere, but I don't know what I can do about it."

"Do you think I'm self-centered and spoiled? That

I just think about having a good time?" Emily's face was serious.

Her mother hesitated before answering. "I wish I could say no," she said. "And I'm not blaming you. I think you are influenced by your friends who have everything, their home computers, VCRs, tapes— you name it, they've got it. You are spoiled, but it's hard not to spoil kids. We can't pretend to be poor when we're not. The thing is not to let those material things take over and be all-important. I don't want you to be aimless. It's time for you to start to think about what you want to do with your life. You can't be sixteen forever, you've got to start to think about what you want to make of yourself."

"I know," Emily said. But those were just words. She didn't really know. She liked her life, she liked having a good time. She liked having new clothes, having money for the movies and eating out, for making out a long Christmas list and getting everything on it. But so far she hadn't had to work for any of it. Suddenly it was beginning to dawn on Emily that a free ride couldn't go on forever.

When she left her mother, she felt frightened. No one was really safe. What if she were struck down like Joey before she had a chance to be someone more than a spoiled sixteen-year-old kid? In her room she looked around at all her possessions: her four-poster bed with its ruffled skirt, her pine desk and chair, the colorful handwoven rugs, her books and knickknacks, her stereo and dozens of tapes and records. She had wanted them so badly and they had seemed so important, but now she wondered why she had ever thought she couldn't live without them.

Of course she was spoiled, there was no doubt about it, but that didn't mean she had to be aimless and selfish as the newspaper described. She resolved to do some serious thinking.

Emily felt more sympathetic to Russ when she called him. He hadn't been as analytical as her mother, but he had been aware of the town's smugness in a way that she, herself, had not. Perhaps she should redo her thinking about his friendship with Danny. It could be a good thing. She had better watch herself, she thought, and be more open and tolerant, not make such quick, harsh judgments.

Russ seemed glad to hear from her and a date was set up.

On Friday night, getting ready to go out with Russ, Emily felt almost normal for the first time since the accident. She was determined not to think about the tragedy, not to be judgmental about Russ or his friends, and to try her best to have a good time. Her parents were delighted to see her going out, and when Russ arrived, they gave him a warm welcome.

"You look gorgeous." Russ's admiring glance took in Emily's long denim skirt, her scoop-necked loose black sweater, and her long gold earrings.

"She does look pretty good, doesn't she?" Mr. Simpson agreed, eyeing his daughter proudly. "Takes after her old man," he added with a grin.

"She looks just like her mother," Russ retorted.

"Thank you kindly." Mrs. Simpson kissed Emily and Russ good-bye. "Have a good time. And, of course, no driving and drinking."

"Don't worry. That's a given," Russ assured them. "None of us are old enough to get served, anyway."

It was the first time Emily had driven with Russ since the accident, but after a few uneasy minutes she sat back in her seat and felt okay. They picked up Becky and Hank and headed for the Valley Pub, which was about forty-five minutes away.

The pub was crowded with young people since there was a popular band there that night, but after a fifteen-minute wait they were given a small table in a corner of the room. Russ had been willing to stand at the crowded bar, but the girls vetoed that.

They ordered sodas and sat down to listen to the music. There was no floor for dancing. The pub was truly a pub, a place to come to eat and drink and, on weekends, to listen to the music. It wasn't a good place for conversation, either. The room had dark, wood-paneled walls, the tables were close together, and even though the band was in the adjoining room near the bar, the noise made talking almost impossible.

"I sure would like a beer," Russ said. "This drinking law gets me mad. My parents let me drink a beer at home. I don't see why I can't have one when I'm out."

"It's supposed to cut down on drinking and driving," Becky said.

"It doesn't keep kids from drinking at home." Hank was on Russ's side.

Emily was only half listening to the conversation. She thought the noise and all the people oppressive and was wondering what she was doing there. And she still felt uncomfortable with Russ. His reaction to the accident was so different from hers, and he had never allowed them a chance to talk about it together.

It wasn't only Russ. She sensed a distance growing between herself and the others. She listened idly as the conversation turned from drinking beer to VCRs and the variations among them, to renting movies, to Christmas vacation plans. It all sounded so trivial and insignificant. She didn't want to be a heavy and go around taking life *seriously*, but sitting here, among the noise and chatter, she felt restless and bored. But why? She had never felt this way before with her friends. It was as if, out of the senselessness of Joey's death, Emily suddenly felt she had to give her own life some meaning.

"You're very quiet," Russ said to her after a while.

"I've got a headache," Emily lied. "I'm sorry."

"It is noisy here," Becky said. "Maybe we should go."

"No, I like it." Russ ordered more sodas.

"I'm ready to leave," Hank said to Becky. "But Russ is driving."

"I guess you're stuck," Russ said with a grin. "Come on, relax. The music's great."

"It's loud enough," Becky muttered.

Emily could feel the evening falling apart. Russ was tapping out the beat of the music with his fingers on the table, Becky and Hank were talking softly to each other, and she was just staring in front of her. She saw Russ look up suddenly, and she followed his eyes to see Chet walk in. She was surprised to see him there. He was alone and stood at the bar. His sensitive, intelligent face, with his dark, brooding eyes, stood out from the crowd. Emily wished she could go over and talk to him, but she didn't dare.

Nervously she watched Russ staring at Chet. She was afraid he was going to start something. "Come on, let's go, Russ," she pleaded. "I really do have a bad headache."

"I'll see if I can get you an aspirin," he offered. "I'll ask at the bar."

This was not what she wanted, but he had gotten up and was on his way. He went directly to where Chet was standing. Emily kept her eyes glued on the two boys. She gasped when she watched Russ distinctly push Chet aside to get closer to the bar. "Hank"—she turned to Becky's date imploringly— "please stop Russ from doing anything stupid. He's trying to start a fight with Chet Bernstein."

Hank got up from the table, but he was too late. Russ said something—Emily couldn't hear him— and the next minute Chet socked him in the jaw. In seconds the bartender and a heavy six-footer at the bar had hold of the two boys and threw them both out the door. "Get out and stay out," the bartender yelled after them. "No fighting around here."

Emily ran to the door with Hank and Becky close behind her. It was very dark outside, and it took Emily a few seconds to see anything. Then she heard a car starting up and saw Russ at the wheel. His headlights caught Emily and the two others.

"Hey," Hank yelled. "Where're you going?"

"I was going to drive around for a while. I was coming back for you," Russ said, leaning out his window. His face was streaked with blood.

"I hope so. Wait, we'll all go home. Come on, Emily." Hank had Becky's hand and opened the back door of the car.

"Where's Chet? What happened to him?" Emily asked.

"Who cares? Come on." Russ had his foot on the accelerator.

Emily looked around the parking lot, lit up by Russ's headlights. She saw Chet leaning against a car several cars down. He was holding a handkerchief to his face.

"I'm going to see if he's okay," Emily called out.

"Leave him alone. I'm not waiting," Russ yelled. "If you want a ride home with me, come on."

Emily stood still. Maybe Chet wanted to be left alone, but she wasn't going to go off and just leave him there if he was hurt. Suddenly she didn't want Chet to associate her with Russ and his stupid anger. She wavered for a minute—she was a long way from home, but she'd get a ride from someone. There were other kids there from Hogan's Bridge Farm. "Go ahead," she called to Russ. "I'll get my own ride home."

"Emily, please come," Becky said, leaning out of the window.

"No, go ahead, I'll be okay." Emily watched Russ's car zoom out of the parking lot.

Emily stood uncertainly in the darkness. Chet had not moved from where he had been standing, slouched against the car. He was still holding a cloth to his face, and Emily thought that without the car behind him he would have sunk to the ground. Hesitantly she walked toward him. She didn't know what to expect. He might rebuff her; he might vent his anger with Russ against her. . . . She had to take her chances.

"Chet . . . are you okay?" She approached him cautiously.

He jumped at her voice and took the handkerchief from his face. "Oh, you." His voice was more tired than angry. His face was bloody and filled with pain.

"You're not all right. Where are you hurt?"

"Who knows. It's not your concern, anyway."

"That's for me to decide. Where's your car? I'll drive you home." He looked so hurt, as if he were suffering more than physical pain, that instinctively Emily took charge.

"Where's your boyfriend? Was that his car that pulled out? What'd he do, go off and leave you?"

"I didn't want to go with him. Come on, Chet, you're all bloody, you need some attention." No longer afraid, she took his arm.

"Ouch." He winced when she touched his elbow. "My arm's sore."

"I'm sorry. You sure can't drive, so come on."

Reluctantly he led her to his car and gave her the keys. She got into the driver's seat and Chet got in beside her.

"You gotta pump the gas to get her started," Chet said, and then leaned his head back against the seat. When Emily glanced at him, his eyes were closed. She thought he might be asleep so she remained quiet. She got the car started and drove off.

When she stopped in front of Chet's house, his eyes were open but he didn't move to get out of the car. He sat staring into space. "You okay?" Emily asked.

"I'd like to go someplace to get cleaned up," Chet said. "I don't want my mom to see me this way. She doesn't need this."

"Of course." Emily felt that she should have thought of that herself. "I'll take you to my house."

"You sure that's okay?"

"Certainly."

It was clear that Chet was uncomfortable as he followed Emily into the darkened house. "Is there anybody home? Where are your parents?" He had pulled up the collar of his jacket as if he didn't want anyone to see his face.

"I think they're probably asleep. I'll take you into my bathroom."

Chet stumbled in the hall, and Emily turned on a light. Now she really saw his pale, blood-streaked face. It was a good thing his mother didn't see him this way, she thought, avoiding his eyes burning with pain or rage—she wasn't sure which. "I'll get a cloth so we can wash you off."

She sat him down on the edge of the bathtub and gently patted his face with the damp cloth. He winced when she tried to remove the dried-up blood, but he told her to keep going. Except for the scratches on his face and a rather large, purple bruise on his cheek, he was beginning to look almost normal. Suddenly he turned his face away. To Emily's surprise his eyes were welling up with tears.

"Did I hurt you?"

Chet shook his head. Abruptly he folded his arms on the nearby sink and buried his head. He was convulsed with sobs.

Emily was frightened. "Chet, what is it?"

He kept shaking his head. "This is stupid," he said, still sobbing. "I haven't cried for Joey, and now, here, out of the blue . . . it's ridiculous . . ."

"It's all right, you have a right to cry." She didn't know what to do. Whether to leave him alone, to touch him, to try to comfort him . . . She just stood very still, near him but keeping her arms folded across her chest.

"I feel so stupid, crying here," Chet kept protesting. "Why here, in your bathroom? It's crazy. It's anger as much as anything," he said, finally getting himself under control. "I get so mad when I think about the senselessness. And now to be caught fighting. What are we fighting about? Joey would call us dumb jerks, I can just hear him, the way he'd say it. And we are dumb—you, me, and Russ—and yet when I see Russ, something happens. I boil up so, I want to choke him. Sometimes I think I'm losing my mind." He looked at her seriously. "Do you think I'm going crazy?"

"No, I don't." Emily answered him with the same seriousness. "We've all been hit hard. How is your mother?" she asked abruptly.

"Awful." Chet splashed water over his face and stood up. "I'd better go home. She'll be worrying. She worries now every time I go out in the car. She won't go near a car—hasn't been in one since the accident. It's been hard on my father. He loved Joey, too, but he has his work. She has nothing."

"She has you." Emily felt close to tears herself.

"It's not the same. Joey was her baby."

"Come on, I'll drive you home." Emily turned out the light and led him into the hall.

"I'll walk," Chet said. "I could use the air. I'll pick up the car tomorrow. Thanks, Emily. I'm sorry I made a fool of myself."

"Don't be ridiculous. I think crying was good for you."

"Yeah, but not in your bathroom." He gave her a weak smile. "Good night." Suddenly he bent down and kissed her cheek. "You're okay," he said, and went out the door.

Emily watched him walk down the street toward his house. She touched her cheek tentatively. His kiss had taken her by surprise, but her own reaction surprised her even more. She was filled with a warmth, the same feeling as catching someone's eye across a room and knowing that in that moment your thoughts and feelings had meshed. She wondered if Chet had felt it as strongly as she had.

When Russ telephoned Emily the next day, Emily told her mother that she didn't want to talk to him. "I'm finished with Russ," Emily called to her mother from her own room. "Tell him anything you like. Tell him I've gone to the moon."

"What happened?" Her mother came into her room after hanging up the phone. "He sounded very upset."

"I don't care. It's his own fault." She told her mother what had happened the night before.

"That's too bad. I feel sorry for him." Mrs. Simpson was sitting on Emily's bed with a sympathetic expression on her face, watching Emily pick up her clothes from chairs and the floor and hang them up. "He's as upset as you are about Joey. Remember, he was driving. Don't be so hard on him."

"I'm not. But he's behaving badly. You're always excusing people. Honestly, Mom, you never find anything wrong with anyone."

Her mother laughed. "You'd be surprised. I find plenty wrong if I see it. But just because Russ is reacting differently from you, you criticize him. You're hard on that friend of his too."

Emily shook her head. "I don't think so. Just because Danny lives on the wrong side of town you forgive him anything. Being poor doesn't justify acting like a nerd."

"I never said it did. But it's too easy for people who have everything to condemn those who don't. I don't even know why you think Danny's what you call a nerd, whatever that is. What has he done that's so terrible?"

Emily looked at her mother curiously. She tried to think of the right answer, then shook her head impatiently. "There's no one thing. He just hangs around. He's not supposed to have any money, but he seems to have enough to drink with, and as far as I know, he doesn't have a job. I think he's a bum."

"But you don't know," her mother persisted.

"Maybe friends buy him drinks, maybe he can't get a job. . . . You get an impression because he's not from your background and decide he's no good. I don't want you to grow up to be a snob, Emily. I worry about that."

"I'm *not* a snob," Emily said indignantly. "I don't understand you. Most mothers wouldn't want their daughters to be seen with Danny, and you're telling me to be nice to him."

Her mother laughed. "I'm not telling you to go out with him if you don't like him. I'm just saying not to make quick, harsh judgments when you don't know the facts."

"Okay, I get the message." Emily, aware of her own resolution to be more tolerant, felt confused. While she admired her mother and her mother's principles, she felt Mrs. Simpson was too accepting of others. She seemed to let Emily's father dominate her too much. It seemed that lately her parents had been arguing more, and it disturbed Emily. The big debate going on now between her parents was what they were going to do Christmas Eve. One of her father's important clients was giving a big party that he wanted to attend, while her mother said that Christmas Eve was a time to stay home. Her mother talked a lot about the family parties they had had when she was a child, when all the cousins and aunts and uncles came on Christmas Eve and put their presents under the tree, and everyone sat around the piano singing Christmas carols. "The people who worked on the farm came in, and our neighbors, the postmistress, the minister, the owners of the village store, everyone dropped in for hot cider and cookies. It was an old-fashioned Christmas and that's what it should be like," her mother had said.

But Christmas was still weeks away, and Emily didn't want to get involved in their arguments, nor did she want to talk about Russ and Danny. It was Chet Bernstein who was on her mind. She wasn't naive enough to give any meaning to his light kiss. He had only been saying thank-you for helping him out. His car was gone when she got up, and there was no word from him, yet she kept thinking about him. Looking back, it now seemed odd to her that although she'd been baby-sitting for Joey since she was thirteen, she'd had so few conversations with Chet. He had always seemed unapproachable, even when he was younger. Many times he'd been home when she came to take care of Joey, but he had kept to himself. In the wintertime he'd stay up in his room building something with his tools or playing his records; in the summer, if he wasn't out walking in the woods, he'd be practicing basket shots behind their house. Emily felt as if he had never even looked at her—she was just someone who'd come in to take care of his baby brother. Last night, she felt, was the first time he'd really seen her.

Her reaction was mixed: If he couldn't bear the sight of her because of her connection with Joey and his death, he certainly didn't show it last night. Yet her feeling of elation had little foundation. Nothing had happened except that she had brought him home and he appreciated that. She was dopey to give any importance to a light kiss, but all the same, she kept thinking about how she could get to know him better.

A few days later Emily announced to her mother that she was going to visit Mrs. Bernstein. She told herself that it was not because of Chet—there was every reason in the world why she should go to see Joey's mother, especially since Chet had told her what a bad time she was having. Emily knew, from the past, that Mrs. Bernstein was fond of her, and also that she was not a woman with many friends. She was a private person, which had made her affection for Emily all the more precious. If Emily stayed away now, after Mrs. Bernstein's first shock and mourning were over, she would have reason to be hurt. Fortified with this rationale, Emily faced her mother for her reaction.

"If you think she would like to see you," Mrs. Simpson said, "by all means go."

Emily kept thinking about the visit and putting it off, wanting to do it but feeling nervous about actually going to the Bernstein house unannounced. After all, her last visit hadn't been at all pleasant. Yet she knew she didn't want to telephone first because she didn't know what to say on the phone; she just wanted to drop in casually.

It took her almost a week to get up her courage, but on Friday afternoon after school, she walked the familiar blocks to their house and rang the bell.

Mrs. Bernstein answered the door, and if she was surprised to see Emily, she didn't show it. She greeted her with a kiss on her cheek as she always had and asked her in. Emily was the one who felt strange. She realized that she was waiting to hear Joey come bouncing down the stairs, and knowing that she would never hear him again, she wanted to run out of the house. However, she followed Mrs. Bernstein into the family den where Mrs. Bernstein spent a lot of her time. The small room was lined with books and was cozy with a fireplace, a small sofa, a few chairs, and Mrs. Bernstein's desk. Emily never knew what Joey's mother did there, but she had heard her laughingly say that very often she did nothing. "I read, write letters, look out the window, just sit. I'm like some primitive people who are never impatiently waiting; when they sit, they are simply living."

She was a quiet, composed woman, and like her son Chet, she had a certain remote quality. Without being cold, she was reserved, indicating that although she might respond, the other person had to make the first move in her direction.

Mrs. Bernstein had Emily sit down on the settee beside her, and spoke easily as if it were customary for Emily to be visiting her. She asked about school and about Emily's parents, but all the while they were talking, Emily had the feeling that the older woman had something else on her mind. After a short while she stood up, a slim figure in a long, dark wool skirt and a heavy, turtle-necked sweater, and said, "Would you like to go up to Joey's room?"

Emily was taken aback by the question. "W-well, yes, if you want to," she said, stammering.

Mrs. Bernstein looked relieved and happy. "Come on." She took Emily by the arm and, almost gaily, led her up the stairs to her dead son's room.

The room was exactly as Emily remembered it. She was shocked to see large wooden blocks on the floor where she and Joey had been playing with them a couple of days before the accident. The bed had his stuffed panda and teddy bear against the pillows, and an unfinished jigsaw puzzle was still on his small desk. The room had not been touched, except, Emily noticed, no dust had accumulated. Mrs. Bernstein must clean it every day.

Joey's mother sat down on a low rocker near the window and motioned Emily to a large, floppy, yellow hassock. "You often sat on that, didn't you?"

Emily nodded and sank down, fitting neatly into the impression left by her own body. The hassock was comfortable, but she did not relax. Her body was taut, the strain of what was taking place pulling at her, as if she were a puppet with someone else holding and controlling the strings. She didn't know what motions she was going to be expected to make.

"You don't mind being here, do you?" Mrs. Bernstein asked softly. "I find it very peaceful."

The late-afternoon sun was lighting up the casement windows above Mrs. Bernstein's chair, giving a pinkish glow to her face, and she did look peaceful. The strained lines and the dark circles under her eyes seemed ironed out, perhaps by some trick of the light, but her face looked younger and more alive.

"I don't mind," Emily whispered, feeling that any loud noise would shatter something fragile in the room. She felt panicky, afraid that Mrs. Bernstein might do something bizarre, such as try to communicate with Joey. Yet there was a serenity in the room that she could feel, as if everything there were at rest and would remain that way forever.

"I come here every afternoon." Mrs. Bernstein spoke in a low, confidential tone. "My husband doesn't like it. He thinks it's morbid but it's not. I don't feel morbid here. It's the only time of the day—or night—that I feel peaceful, that I have any rest. It's as if I were visiting with Joey—I'm not crazy, I don't believe in the supernatural, yet I feel his presence here. And why not? All his things are here, even the delicious smell of him is here. Some people visit graves but I don't like that. That, to me, would be morbid. I don't want to think of Joey in a grave, but here I can think of him alive, and if I can't hold on to that image of him, I would die. Do you think I'm crazy?"

"No, of course not. I—I think Joey would like you to be here." Emily hesitated. "I'm flattered that you asked me to sit here with you."

Mrs. Bernstein looked happy. "What a nice thing to say. You were so close to Joey, he loved you. I was hoping you would come to see me. I've thought about you and that boy who was driving the car. I don't feel the way my husband and Chet do—I've felt so sorry for you—it must be so hard for that boy. However it happened, it was nothing he *wanted* to do. What can be worse than to have to live the rest of his life remembering those horrible few minutes? His pain must be terrible. Is he suffering terribly?"

"I don't know," Emily said. Mrs. Bernstein made her feel guilty, but she looked at the woman opposite her with awe. *She* was worried about Russ; she was feeling sorry for Russ. It seemed incredible, and yet maybe Russ was suffering, maybe he was behaving the way he did to cover up his own hurting.

They sat quietly, watching the light change the colors of the room. When the sun was almost gone, beyond the hills outside of the town, Emily got up and said she had to go home. "This was lovely." Mrs. Bernstein sighed. "Will you come again? Oh, dear, I should have made tea or offered you a soda and cookies. I didn't think of it." She shook her head. "I'm so sorry."

"I didn't want anything, honestly."

Downstairs Mrs. Bernstein took Emily's hands in both of hers. "Please come back, I'm always here. Perhaps," she said, and looked at Emily shyly, "perhaps we could play some of Joey's games or finish painting his desk. Remember, you were going to help him finish painting it when he decided whether he wanted to keep it white or make it red. I've thought about it but never got up the energy to do it alone. If you helped me . . . ?"

"If you'd like me to, of course."

"You don't think I'm crazy, do you?" Mrs. Bernstein's eyes were searching her face.

"No, I don't think you're crazy," Emily said firmly and deliberately. Now, in a different light, the older woman's face looked so sad, Emily thought. Even if she was flaky, it didn't matter. If being in Joey's room helped her, so what?

She was about to open the door when Chet came in. He looked at her with surprise.

"Emily's been visiting me," his mother said quickly. "Isn't that nice?"

"I guess so. If you enjoyed it," he added in a warmer voice. "It's better than—" He stopped and flushed, embarrassed.

" 'Better than sitting in Joey's room,' you wanted to say." Mrs. Bernstein laughed. "You can say it, I don't care. But that's what we did do. Emily and I. I think she's going to be a big help to me—that is, if she doesn't mind." She turned to Emily with a happy, warm smile. "I do appreciate your coming. It means a lot to me." She gave her son the kind of look a child might give to his mother, afraid of getting scolded. "Emily doesn't think I'm crazy—I think she understands."

"I hope I do," she said warmly, and gave her cheek to Mrs. Bernstein for her kiss. "Good-bye."

Emily walked quickly down the path from their front door, and then slowed down when she got to the street. It was almost dark, although not quite five o'clock. She'd been with Mrs. Bernstein only since around half past three, but she felt as if she had lived through some momentous experience, as if a remote Mrs. Bernstein had taken her into a private world of her own. Walking along the blocks to her own house, she welcomed the sturdy reality of the familiar streets and houses.

After that initial visit, Emily made it a habit to go see Mrs. Bernstein as often as she could. As far as Joey's mother was concerned, she would have been happy to have Emily come there every day. She was filled with plans for the two of them: They would paint the desk; they would play with Joey's board games, work on his puzzles; they would make cookies, watch Joey's television shows. . . . She was building a life for herself and Emily.

On her part, Emily's feelings were mixed. She truly liked Mrs. Bernstein and wanted to help her. She had a genuine affection for Joey's mother and also felt an obligation to do what she could. But she worried about the older woman counting on her too heavily. Her friends at school, Becky in particular, complained that they never saw her anymore. She dropped out of basketball practice, and too many afternoons when Becky asked her to do something together, Emily begged off because she had promised Mrs. Bernstein to be there.

At home Emily became a source of arguments between her parents. Her mother was sympathetic to her friendship with Mrs. Bernstein, but her father objected. "I think it's fine for you to want to help the poor woman," her father said, "but I don't like you spending so much time with her. In the end, I don't think it's going to do her any good. She's not dealing with Joey's death. She's not facing reality."

"What's so great about facing reality?" Emily asked. She and her parents were at the dinner table, finishing their dessert. "If she's happier keeping Joey alive for herself this way, what's wrong with it?"

"Because she will lose contact with her real world. Eventually, she will lose contact with her husband and her other son. I don't think she's being fair to them."

Her father had done his daily running before dinner, and his round cheeks, red from the wind, made her mother look pale beside him. Even without the windburn, he had a healthy, vigorous air that gave a strength and an authority to whatever he said or did.

While Emily felt closer to her mother, she admired her father a great deal and could sympathize with his burning ambition for success. Except that she felt that he already had succeeded—he had a very good law practice, a nice home, a family he seemed to love. Why did he still drive himself so hard? It was that drive not to miss anything, to get every possible new client, to win every case, that Emily knew left her mother out. Her mother wanted a slower, more unhurried, easier life.

It never occurred to Emily to choose which of them was right. She could see them both as separate people. What she did wonder about was what of each was in her own makeup; which genes were stronger? She felt she was more like her mother— she hated competition and as yet had found no great, burning ambition to be someone or to do something *great*, yet there were also times when she was afraid of being a nonentity.

Her desire to be different was part of her attraction to Mrs. Bernstein. Although it worried her, she was flattered by the older woman's growing dependence on her, and pleased by a feeling of being singled out, as if destiny had planned this role especially for her. While Emily's mother had said that she was proud of her daughter for what she was doing and that not every girl would be willing to give so much time to an older woman, Emily took to heart her mother's warning not to blow herself up in her own eyes. She was simply being decent.

"But I don't think Emily can be the one to decide what Mrs. Bernstein should do," Mrs. Simpson said mildly in answer to her husband. "Adele Bernstein's a grown woman, she's not a child. She's obviously doing what she wants to do."

"She's acting like a child," Mr. Simpson said. "I'm not suggesting that she try to forget Joey; of course she never will. But she's living in a fantasy world and taking Emily into it with her."

"It's not hurting me," Emily said. She gave a small laugh. "Maybe a fantasy world is better than the real one."

"That's where you're wrong," her father said sharply. "The real world can be pretty good. Don't turn your back on it."

Emily and her mother exchanged glances. What was the use? their eyes said. He doesn't believe in fantasies, but that doesn't make them wrong.

As Emily found out, Peter Bernstein, Joey and Chet's father, felt the same way that Mr. Simpson did. The first several afternoons that Emily spent with Mrs. Bernstein, she left before Mr. Bernstein came home. But then one day they were sitting on the floor of Joey's room trying to figure out a rather complicated electronic game. "I'd put this aside for him for when he was older," Mrs. Bernstein had explained. "My sister in California had sent it to him. She must have thought he was a genius." Her eyes filled with tears when she glanced at Emily, but neither one said the obvious: that Joey would never play with it now.

Mrs. Bernstein was still teary-eyed when her husband came into the room. He was a tall, slim man with a shock of dark hair streaked with gray. Emily thought he was very good-looking in a professorial way. His forehead jutted out above deep-set eyes; he dressed casually in blue work shirts, sweaters, and tweed jackets; but he did not seem to be a casual person. He was an intense man who noticed everything. Before he even said hello, he darted over to a wall to straighten out a picture. Then he turned to them. "What are you doing on the floor? It's drafty, there are plenty of good tables and chairs downstairs."

"We like it here," Mrs. Bernstein answered simply. "Aren't you home early?"

"Not especially."

"I guess we lost track of time," she said apologetically. "We got involved in trying to figure this one out."

"Why are you doing this, Adele?" Mr. Bernstein's face was filled with pain. "Give up this room, I beg you."

She looked up at him sorrowfully. "I'll never give it up. You can't ask me to do that."

"I can and I am," he pleaded. He looked from her to Emily. "Don't you see what this is doing to her? I'm not blaming you, I know you're being kind to her and I appreciate it. But it's useless. In the end, it will destroy her, destroy all of us."

Emily felt shattered. Mrs. Bernstein had stretched out her hand and taken hold of Emily's. "Don't listen to him," she whispered. "Please don't leave me. I couldn't bear it if you left. You're my closest connection to Joey." She looked up at her husband. "Yes, I mean that. I know you and Chet both loved Joey dearly, but you didn't know him the way Emily and I did. We spent more time with him, we changed his diapers when he was little, we watched him take his first steps, we taught him numbers and the alphabet, we played games with him, we made up stories for him. . . . We have a right to be here. I need Emily now. Please understand."

"I don't understand," he said miserably. "You have another son, you have me—don't we count for anything?" Again he looked from his wife to Emily. "I'm sorry—you shouldn't be part of this and you don't belong here. I know you were just an innocent passenger, but you were in that car, and seeing you doesn't help, it can't help. My wife is pushing out everything real, she's pushing out her grief and her anger, but it won't work. It's there, festering."

Emily stood up. She was frightened, and all she could think of was to get out. The two pain-filled faces avoiding each other's eyes were too much for her. She felt such empathy for both of them, and yet at the same time, they were draining her. She didn't know who was right and who was wrong any longer. "I've got to go home," she said flatly, and left.

Outside, she ran. She was still running when she ran headlong into Chet. He steadied her with his arms. "What's the matter? What happened?"

"Nothing. I was late, that's why I was running."

"You came from my house, didn't you?"

She nodded. "Yes."

"Something happened there. Tell me."

"Nothing, really."

He held her eyes. "I hope you know what you're doing spending so much time with my mother."

"She asks me to," Emily said.

"I know."

"But maybe I won't be doing it so much any-more." Emily searched his face for a clue to his feelings. He was unsmiling, and his face was impassive.

"I have a lot of schoolwork, so I won't be able to come over as much." She wasn't fooling him but he accepted her excuse.

"That may be just as well." He said good-bye and walked past her to his own house.

Emily walked home more slowly. She had spoken without thinking, and she was worried about letting Mrs. Bernstein down. Yet she didn't want to antagonize the rest of the Bernstein family. Emily let out a deep sigh. Poor little Joey . . . his senseless death was causing even wider and deeper ripples of tragedy. Suddenly Emily felt very angry: How dare all these people fight about how to mourn for Joey. She hadn't had time to really understand her own feelings, but right now she was furious: angry at Russ for not being able to stop the car in time; angry at Joey for running out so recklessly; angry at his family; and even angry with her own family. Tragedy, she thought, was supposed to bring families and people together, but the people around Joey were all being splintered apart.

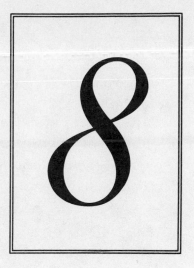

For the first time in her life Emily Jane hated Christmas Eve. She wished she could disappear until the entire Christmas holiday was over. She couldn't stir up any Christmas cheer; she had no interest in making her usual brownies and cookies, or in decorating the tree. She felt she would be happy to pull the covers over her head and wake up when the whole thing was over.

Her parents' moods weren't much better. The morning of Christmas Eve their argument started again or, as Emily surmised, was probably just continuing. She could hear them from her bedroom.

"This party's very important to me," her father was saying. "Not because it's a party—I'm not that big on parties—but it's the people who will be there. It's important that I be seen at the Caldwells' Christmas party."

"If it's a big party, no one will know if you're there or not. I know those parties, you've dragged me to enough of them. Nobody really talks to anyone. I don't know the people, I feel uncomfortable. Besides, Steve, it's Christmas Eve. Doesn't that mean anything to you?"

"A good time to go out," her father said.

"On the contrary. A time to stay home. We never went out on Christmas Eve, except to walk up to the church and sing Christmas carols. We decorated the tree and had a special Christmas Eve dinner. It was family time. I think it would be nice for Emily if we stayed home. She's been having a rough time. . . . Last year we went to a party and I hated it."

Now Emily did pull the covers over her head. She couldn't bear to hear her mother feeling sorry for her. Besides, she didn't want to hear any more. Listening to them made her feel helpless and frustrated, as she couldn't see any way for them to settle their differences. Her father cared about his work, perhaps made that his first priority, while her mother wanted a different kind of life. Emily felt as if their loss was hers, and as if only sadness was running loose around the world. What a terrible way to feel the day before Christmas!

By the time she came downstairs, Mr. Simpson had gone to his office and her mother was still sitting at the breakfast table staring sadly out of the window.

"What are you going to do? Are you going to Dad's party?"

"I suppose so," her mother said, shrugging. "He says it's important."

"You don't have to go. You can stay home."

Mrs. Simpson smiled. "I suppose that's what you would do. But I wouldn't enjoy that, staying home without him."

Emily shrugged. "Are there any happy marriages, Mom?"

Her mother looked startled. "Yes, I'm sure there are many. Don't you think your father and I have a happy marriage?"

Emily looked away from her mother's face. "Not very. You want to live one way and Dad another. I used to think the Bernsteins were the perfect couple, never quarreling. Now, since the accident, they have differences. I don't know . . . ever since Joey's death, everything seems to be going wrong. I wish it wasn't Christmas," she added fiercely. "I hate it."

"I'm sorry. That's a terrible way to feel. I wish I could cheer you up, but I guess I don't feel so cheerful myself." Mrs. Simpson carried a few breakfast dishes from the table to the sink. "You know, I've been thinking. I'd like to go home for a visit, by myself. That is, without your father. Would you like to come?"

"I couldn't. I have school in another week." Emily felt panicky. "Are you thinking of leaving Dad?"

"I don't know. Sometimes I think of it. But I love him. I don't want to leave, but my life here seems so empty."

"How would it feel filled?"

"That's the trouble. I don't know. I think if I lived in the country, had a lot of animals. I think I was meant to be a farmer's wife. Growing food, or a dairy farm—to me they're real, necessary. I'm not putting down what your father does. Lawyers are important, I suppose, but it's not basic."

Emily sat with her hands in her lap, looking at her mother. "I know what you mean. Little Joey's getting killed that way has made me think about a lot of things. I mean, to see his life suddenly ending that way—it hits home more than all the awful tragedies you read about in the papers or see on TV. Everyone, the kids I know, are so busy trying to have a good time. I'm all for having fun, but I want my life to be *real*, to have a meaning. Otherwise the whole thing is useless—I mean, living at all."

"There is so much that is phony and superficial, it's hard to keep in touch with what's real. I think the main thing is to be honest, honest with yourself and your own point of view, your own standards."

"Are you being honest?"

"Not entirely. That's what I have to figure out. That's why I think I need to be alone for a while. I have to know if loving your father is enough and how much I am willing to trade off for it. I'm leaving you out of it because you're going to be grown-up and out of the house in a few years. No matter where I am, we'll always be close. We'll always be friends."

Emily got up and put her arms around her mother. "I love you. You'll never get rid of me."

"I'm more afraid of your getting rid of me someday." Her mother held her close.

"Never."

The day dragged itself out. In the late afternoon it began to snow, and that made Emily feel even sadder. It only served as a reminder of all the good Christmases when the snow had been exciting and made Christmas real. She had loved taking her sled to a nearby hill, as recently as the year before when she had considered herself quite grown-up. Sometimes her parents had gone with her, taking turns going down the hill, and they had come home pink and cold, eager to throw off their damp clothes. Her father would make a fire in the fireplace while she and her mother made a big pot of hot chocolate. When the three of them sat around the fire sipping their hot drinks and eating Christmas cookies, Emily had felt her world was secure. For the moment the shadow of her parents' problems had faded and she couldn't have imagined anything disturbing the tranquillity of their lives. But that was then and this was now, and it was all different.

Her father came home from his office early, and Emily was grateful that neither he nor her mother picked up the argument. Her parents rarely kept up a quarrel. They said what they wanted to say and then shut up, but the strain between them did not disappear. Even in her own room Emily was aware of tension in the house.

About six o'clock Mrs. Simpson knocked on Emily's door. Emily told her to come in. She was stretched out on her bed and hastily picked up the book she hadn't been reading. Her mother gave her an anxious look. "Are you all right?"

"Sure, I'm okay."

"I hate going out and leaving you. Don't you want to call any of your friends?"

"No, I don't think so." Emily had been thinking about the Christmas Eve plans she had made months before. Mrs. Bernstein had asked her if she would be free Christmas Eve to baby-sit with Joey, as traditionally they went to a small party at friends'. "You can invite a couple of friends over if you want," Joey's mother had said. "I know you're not crazy to baby-sit on Christmas Eve." Emily had agreed and planned to ask Russ, Becky, and Becky's current boyfriend. Becky had thought it was a wonderful idea. Emily had never gotten around to asking the boys, and Becky had not mentioned it since the accident.

"I wish you wouldn't just lie in your room this way," her mother said.

"Don't worry about me, I'm all right." Emily sat up and faced her mother. "I'm glad you're going out." Mrs. Simpson had on a long black dress, cut low, and with her gold jewelry she looked very elegant. "You don't look like a farmer's wife," Emily said. "You look fantastic. You'll be the best-looking woman there, wherever you're going."

Her mother smiled. "I doubt it. They're a pretty fancy bunch. Designer gowns, real jewelry. I'm all imitation."

"Don't say that. You don't need all that stuff. Stop putting yourself down, Mom. Just because you don't have some hotshot career doesn't mean a thing."

"I don't even want a hotshot career. Maybe that's my trouble."

Mr. Simpson stuck his head in the door. "Emily, get up and do something. I don't want you moping around here alone all evening. Come on, Viv, we've got to get going."

They both kissed Emily good-bye. "Are you going to get up?" her father asked at the door.

"I don't know. Don't worry about me. Have a good time. Merry Christmas."

"Merry Christmas, darling," her mother said, and followed her father to the door.

When Emily heard the door close behind them, she turned over onto her stomach.

Against her will she started reliving those few moments in the car before she heard Joey's scream. Had she really been as happy as she thought she was? Maybe she was fooling herself and her life had not been all that divine before. Russ had started becoming a problem, differences between her parents had been surfacing . . . The difference was that she had not given the quality of her life much thought. One day had followed another, and she hadn't known, nor cared, where they were heading.

She must have fallen asleep, because the ringing of the telephone woke her with a jolt. She was still half asleep when she pulled her phone from her bedside table and lifted the receiver. "Emily Jane, please." It was a male voice she didn't recognize right away. He sounded in a hurry.

"This is Emily."

"Chet Bernstein. This is a terrible time to call, Christmas Eve, and if you have to say no, I'll understand. But could you come over here for a few minutes—it's an emergency."

"Has something happened?" She felt he was trying to conceal his alarm. Her stomach felt wobbly.

"I'm not sure. Can you come?"

"Yes, of course. I'll be right over."

She didn't do anything but run a comb through her hair and throw on her brown down coat. She ran the few blocks to the Bernstein house. The house was blazing with lights.

Chet must have been watching out for her, and he opened the door before she rang the bell. His white face told her that something certainly had happened.

"What is it?"

"My mother. My parents had an argument—I hate bringing you into this, but I thought you could help. My dad went out, and my mother's locked herself in Joey's room and won't come out. I'm worried sick. She has a bunch of pills—the doctor gave her something for sleeping. I don't know if she has them in there with her or not, but I'm scared. I thought maybe you could get her to open the door."

"I can try." Emily followed him to just outside of Joey's room. There was no sound from inside.

"Mrs. Bernstein," Emily called softly. "I came over to say hello. My folks went out and I was alone. I thought I could sit with you for a while."

She heard a slight sound of someone moving, but there was no answer. "Please, Mrs. Bernstein, please let me in. I'd like to be with you. It's Christmas Eve and I was feeling lonely. I won't bother you. You don't have to talk if you don't want to. Just let me in."

There was a long silence. Then, in a weak voice, Mrs. Bernstein said, "Who's out there with you?"

"Chet is here, that's all. He let me in."

"Tell him to go away."

"Okay." Chet's face hardened and he bit his lip. "I'll leave," he whispered.

Emily shook her head. "Please stay close . . . don't leave the house."

"I'll be in the TV room," he told her, and walked away.

"I'm alone," Emily said to the closed door. "May I come in now?" Her heart was thumping against her chest as she heard the key turn in the lock. She didn't know what she would find when the door opened.

Mrs. Bernstein looked terrible. Her face was ashen; her hair, usually glossy and neat, was hanging in disarray; and she was clasping and unclasping her hands nervously. She grabbed hold of Emily's hand and held it tight. "I'm a mess," she said. "I'm falling apart and I can't stop myself. I don't know what to do. . . . I don't think I can go on living. No one understands how I feel. I'm not sure even you do. My beautiful little boy. I keep seeing him maimed, crushed. . . . I want to do something terrible, to kill someone, and the only one I can kill is myself. There is no place I can find any peace."

"I think I do know how you feel," Emily said softly. "Everyone has been hurt by Joey's death. It's been horrible. But don't hurt them more, please. Mr. Bernstein loves you, Chet loves you, I love you . . . it would be a terrible thing, terrible for Joey, if there was more tragedy. You're bound to feel better sometime. Think of the games we've played here together. . . ."

"But they don't want me to do that anymore. My husband wants me to change this room, he wants me to get rid of Joey. I think he wants me to forget Joey."

"Oh, no. I'm sure he doesn't. No one's ever going

to forget Joey. But maybe you have to remember him kind of inside yourself. I mean, maybe you don't need his room or all his things to remember him." Emily looked at the older woman and thought that for the first time she, herself, was able to think of Joey as being dead. Yes, he had lived and now he was dead, as everyone would have to be someday. There was no changing that, no fighting it. Maybe that was what made life so precious. Being alive—and doing something with that life—was what counted, and Mrs. Bernstein had forgotten that. Emily's father was right. Instead of Joey's death giving his mother a stronger hold on life, wanting to give more to Chet and her husband, she was folding up inward, turning away from life.

Suddenly, Emily wished she could shake this sad, intelligent woman, make her wake up to what she was doing, make her see that she was negating the memory of her bright, lively little son.

"Come on." She gently pulled Mrs. Bernstein in the direction of the door. "Chet is very upset and it's Christmas Eve. Let's go see what he's doing."

Mrs. Bernstein shrank back. "No, I'd rather stay here. I feel close to Joey when I'm here. I can't leave him alone on Christmas Eve."

"Joey's not here," Emily said firmly.

Mrs. Bernstein stared at her, wide-eyed. "Of course he's here. I can even smell him. You think I'm crazy but I'm not. His spirit is here, it's in all his things, his toys, his bed, his clothes—his presence is here. I'm not talking about a ghost, I don't believe in ghosts. But there is such a thing as a soul. I can feel it, can't you?"

Before this evening Emily would have gone along with Mrs. Bernstein, would have meekly agreed that yes, she felt Joey's presence too. But now she was reaching for the truth, for reality for herself as well as for the older woman. "No, I don't feel anything," she said. "This room is sad, it's like living through Joey's death over and over again. There's no sense to it. You're alive, Chet's alive, your husband is alive. *They* need you, this room doesn't. Come on, please."

She practically pulled Mrs. Bernstein from the room and led her down the hall to where Chet was sitting, staring at the picture on TV. He had turned on the television without the sound, and it was eerie to watch a choral group open and close their mouths without a peep coming out. He stood up when his mother and Emily came into the room, and switched off the set. He seemed embarrassed, as if he didn't know what to say, but he gave Emily a grateful smile.

"Come sit down. Can I get you something?" he asked his mother. "How about a glass of sherry or some tea? Would you like that?"

"I don't think so. I feel very tired. I think I'll go to my room and lie down. You two can celebrate Christmas Eve if you like." She said it as if it were the last thing in the world she could imagine anyone wanting to do.

"Can I do anything?" Emily asked.

"No, thank you. I'm really all right. I wish people would just leave me alone. I have a right to mourn for my son," she said fiercely.

"Of course you have," Chet said quietly. "But there's a time when even that should end."

"Maybe." She gave him a pained look and abruptly left.

Chet sank back on his chair wearily. "Thanks for getting her to come out. It was lousy to ask you over here on Christmas Eve." He glanced up at her. "Hope it didn't spoil your plans."

"I didn't have any plans," Emily said.

They sat in silence for several minutes. Emily felt that she should get up and leave, yet she didn't want to. She felt as if it was right for her to be sitting there quietly with Joey's brother. As if an invisible web were holding her there.

Finally Chet said, "It's a lousy world, isn't it? There doesn't seem to be much sense to anything."

"I think there's got to be. I don't know what it is, but if everything is just chaos, nothing has any meaning."

"Maybe nothing has. Maybe we'll all get blown up by a nuclear bomb—that would prove there is no meaning."

"It would only prove we're a bunch of jerks. I don't think we are. Listen, if civilization's developed the brains to invent nuclear power, we should have the sense not to use it to destroy the world. It's up to us." Emily spoke vehemently.

"Yeah, yeah, three cheers. You should have a soapbox."

"You can laugh at me, but it's true."

"So what are you doing about it if it's up to us?"

Emily flushed. "Nothing much, I'm afraid. I don't know what to do. But I'll figure out something when I get older. Vote for the right people, for one thing. People who don't want to rule the world with guns. I'll find out what to do."

"Well, right now I'm not out to save the world. I've got too much to worry about right here. Maybe my parents will bust up, maybe my mother's going off her rocker. I've got my own problems."

"I know, I'm sorry. My parents aren't getting along, either."

"They're the ones who are wrecking the world. Half my class has divorced parents. It'll be a long time before I ever get married."

"Me too."

Chet looked up and their eyes met. Then they both laughed. "Boy, we sound like a pair of sad sacks," Chet said. "But you know, when I'm not feeling sorry for myself, I get mad. I feel sorry for my mother but I get mad at her too. Sometimes I wish Joey had never been born." He looked at Emily warily. "You can hate me for saying that, but it's true. We were a very happy family before. I'm not blaming Joey, it wasn't his fault and he was adorable. That was part of the trouble. My mother flipped for him. I think he was a real surprise. My mother didn't expect to have any more kids, and then he came along. He became the apple of her eye. She lived for Joey. She didn't give a hang about me anymore, and not much for my father. Her life revolved around the baby. That's why she's taking this so hard. But that leaves my dad and me out of it. I don't know what's going to happen to us." He stared into space moodily. "Heck, I don't know why I'm telling you all this.

I've never said this to anyone before. But sometimes you seem like one of the family."

"It's okay," Emily said. "You can tell me anything you want. I don't talk."

"What's happened to your boyfriend, Russ?" Chet asked abruptly.

"I don't know. I hardly ever see him."

Chet's dark eyes flashed her a surprised look. "I didn't realize you two had broken up. I think about him a lot. I'd hate to be in his shoes. I wouldn't want to live with what he's living with."

"I thought you hated him," Emily said.

"I do in a way, but I also feel sorry for him. How come you don't see him?"

It was Emily's turn to be surprised. "I don't like the people he's hanging around with, guys like that Danny Porchak."

"What's the matter with Danny? He's okay. He makes furniture for my father. He copies Shaker pieces. They're beautiful."

"*Danny Porchak?* You're kidding. I thought he was a bum."

"You thought wrong. He helps support his folks with his furniture. Maybe he goes out and has a few beers too many once in a while, but so what? That doesn't make him a bum. Just because he lives in a poor part of town and his family's been on welfare doesn't make him a bum. You talk about saving the world and you're a snob."

"I'm not a snob," Emily said indignantly. "At least, I hope I'm not," she added in a milder voice. "I just didn't know."

"Okay, forget it. I'll take you around to Danny's place sometime and show you his stuff. You'll be surprised."

"I'd like that." Emily stood up. "I guess I better go home. I hope your mother will be all right. Call me anytime if you need me. I don't mind."

Chet stood up too. "I'll walk you home. I really gave you an earful tonight. Hope you weren't too bored."

"Not at all." Emily gave him a big smile. "We both opened up, so we're even."

"Yeah." Chet smiled too. He looked as if he wanted to say something more but changed his mind.

"It's been a nice evening," Emily said. "Interesting."

"I'll check on my mother and make sure she's okay. Be with you in a jiffy." Chet left the room and came back in a few minutes. "She's sleeping like a baby," he said.

They walked home in silence, but Chet took her

hand and held it all the way. When they got to her house, he said, "Thank you for coming over," and bent down and gave her a quick kiss on the cheek. He walked away quickly and left her with a quick heartbeat, wishing that she had kissed him back.

It didn't feel like Christmas morning. The presents were under the tree as usual. Emily had put hers there the day before, and her parents must have put theirs down after they had come home from the party. It seemed all three of them were trying to make it a typical family Christmas, exclaiming enthusiastically over their presents, yet at the same time looking to each other for reassurance—as if to say, "Everything's okay, isn't it?"

Emily truly loved the oversized sweater from her mother, the tapes and books from her father, and the beautiful gold watch from both her parents. There were gifts from other relatives and two pairs of wild knee socks from Becky. Last year Joey had made a painting for her. She wished she hadn't thrown it away, but she had when he'd told her he was going to make a better one for her this Christmas.

Her mother fixed their usual festive Christmas breakfast, fresh corn bread, sausage and pancakes, cheeses and coffee.

"How was the party?" Emily asked while they were eating.

"It was all right," her mother said.

Mr. Simpson gave his wife an amused glance. "It was better than that. Your mother was a hit. Don't you know her? She says she hates parties, but when she gets there, she has a wonderful time. All the men flirt with her."

"Don't believe a word he says," her mother said, flushing. "Just because I'm a good sport doesn't mean I'm having a marvelous time."

"But you did enjoy yourself, didn't you?" Her husband looked at her questioningly.

"You're not going to force me to say I loved it," she said with a laugh. "I did it for you." She gave him a mischievous smile.

"That's good enough for me."

Their conversation made Emily feel better. At least they were teasing each other, and that was a good sign. She wondered if her mother still wanted to go home alone, but she wasn't going to ask. Maybe her mother would forget about that.

The day passed quietly, and Emily was glad when it was over. She had spent a good deal of time wondering if she should call to see how Mrs. Bernstein was. But she felt shy about talking to Chet; in fact, she was hoping that he would call her. But he didn't phone, and she let the day go by without calling his house.

A few days later Chet did call, the Saturday before the end of their Christmas vacation. "I'm driving over to Danny's to pick up something for my father. I thought maybe you'd like to come to see what he does."

"I'd love to," Emily said promptly.

When she told her mother where she was going, Mrs. Simpson was surprised. "I thought you didn't like Danny."

Emily flushed. She didn't tell her mother that although she was interested in finding out about Danny Porchak, she was just as interested in getting to know Chet better.

Chet picked her up in the family station wagon. "Danny refinished a cabinet for my father," Chet explained in the car. "This isn't one of Danny's own pieces, just something he restored. But I hope he has something in his barn so you can see what he does. He doesn't often have much around because he sells them or he does something on order. My father tries to give him as much business as he can from his clients. He thinks he's terrific."

"I had no idea Danny did anything like this. He seemed like someone who just hung around doing nothing."

"Well, he's not. I think he works a lot at night because he likes to. He's an oddball guy, but he's a great craftsman. His father was a carpenter and cabinetmaker before he went to work in a factory. But since he's been out of a job, he's a mess. Just sits around the house. Danny and his mother make whatever money they have. His father is in some kind of a depression, and Danny doesn't know when he'll come out of it."

"That must be lousy for them." Emily saw that they had left the nice part of town, crossed the railroad tracks, and turned down Railroad Street. They went past a couple of crummy-looking bars, a small grocery store, an outlet clothing place, and then came to a street of tiny houses. A few of them had plastic sheets covering the glass, for want of storm windows, and most of them had broken front steps and littered front yards. At the end of the block,

Chet pulled into the driveway of a small frame house that was comparatively neat. It was shadowed by a larger barn standing in back of it. A worn truck was parked in front of the barn.

"Good, he's home," Chet said. "He doesn't have a phone. He can get messages at a neighbor's, but I don't like to bother them."

Chet led Emily directly to the barn. Without knocking, he pulled open a wide door and he and Emily quickly stepped inside. Thin walls closed off the room they came into from the rest of the barn, comfortably warm from a wood stove set close to an outside wall through which a thick black pipe cut to the outdoors. A long workbench ran along one wall, and the rest of the room was taken up with lethal-looking machine tools, cut lumber of various lengths and widths, hand tools neatly hung up on a wall, and one high stool on which Danny was perched in front of the workbench. He swung around as Chet closed the outside door. He greeted Chet with a wide smile and stared at Emily.

Danny was a tall, lanky boy with a lot of reddish-brown hair that he held back from his face with a red bandanna folded into a headband. He had on a sweatshirt and faded jeans, sneakers with holes, and no socks. His face was thin, the skin pulled tightly over high cheekbones, the bone structure clearly defined. His features were sharply cut, like a piece of sculpture, and strong. His eyes, looking Emily up and down, were very blue and inquisitive.

"This is Emily Simpson. Perhaps you two know each other," Chet said.

"We've seen each other around." Danny had a slight accent, as if he had grown up in the South.

"Hi," Emily said.

"You come for that cabinet for your father?" Danny asked. "It's back in the barn. I don't have room to keep much stuff in here."

"Yes. Also came by to see you. I wanted to show Emily what you do. Hope you have some things around."

"She doesn't want to see any of my stuff," Danny said. He was still sitting on his stool, his long legs wound around the rungs. "Sorry I don't have any chairs for you to sit on."

"We don't need any," Chet said. "But she does want to. Can we go in back?"

Danny didn't move. He was still looking at Emily. "I don't know why you came here," he said to her. "According to my friend Russ," he said, emphasizing the word *my*, "you think I'm a bum. Well, to tell you the truth, I don't much care for you, either. I think maybe Chet made a mistake bringing you here."

Emily was shocked. To be snubbed by Danny was the last thing she had expected. "That's okay with me. I'm ready to go. I'll wait for you outside, Chet." She turned to go.

Chet looked from one to the other. "What in heck is going on? What have you got against Emily?" he demanded of Danny. "What'd she ever do to you? She just didn't know you."

"I don't care about me. But I don't like the way she dumped Russ. She's acted like he was a criminal. You think it's fun to be driving a car that knocks down a little innocent kid? And not even know how it happened? She was in the car with him, she shoulda stuck with him. They were in it together. He needed every friend he had, but she picks that time to tell him to get lost. You ain't seen Russ the way I have, that boy's been hurting."

"Who said I dumped Russ? He's been avoiding me more than I've avoided him." Emily's eyes were blazing. "I called him up to go out, and maybe he didn't tell you what happened. He got into a fistfight with Chet for no good reason and drove off leaving Chet a mess. He should have bent over backward to be decent to Chet instead of beating him up. Don't tell me about Russ's hurting. How do you think Chet feels—or me, either?"

Chet stared at her in amazement. "Gee, I thought you were on Russ's side."

"I'm on nobody's side," Emily said, still angry. "But what's fair is fair. Come on." She turned to Chet. "I think we'd better go."

Danny, too, was staring at her as if, in spite of himself, he had to admire her standing up to him. "Maybe I didn't have all the facts," he said in his slow drawl. "Maybe, like you say, Russ didn't know how to act with Chet. I mean, he's not the kind to go up to a guy and say, 'I'm sorry about your little brother.' He can feel it but not know how to put it into words. Russ keeps a lot of stuff bottled up, and sometimes it comes out in a fight because he doesn't know what else to do."

"You make him sound like an awful dope," Emily said coldly. "I always thought he had some brains."

"He has," Danny said. "But that's got nothing to do with it. A guy can be smart and still be mixed up." He gave Chet a glance. "Russ has been awful upset about that accident. He doesn't really believe it was his fault, but he keeps tormenting himself with it. You gotta have some pity for the guy."

Emily was at the door but she didn't go out. Instead, she said to Danny, "He's got a good friend in you. I owe you an apology. I thought you were a bum and turning Russ into one too. I guess I was wrong. But that doesn't change anything. Everyone's been hurt by that horrible accident, but it's how people behave that counts. For Russ to go around drinking and feeling sorry for himself and fighting with Chet doesn't help anyone. I feel sorry for him."

Danny gave her an amused smile. "I'll give him the message."

Emily flushed. "Thanks," she said. "I hope you do. And I don't give a darn if you're laughing at me. I loved Joey and I was in the car, but I'm going to be all right. I owe it to Joey to be okay and better than okay. You can tell that to Russ too." She walked out of the barn.

Chet came out after her. "Do you want to see Danny's stuff?" he asked. "After all, that's what you came for. . . ."

Emily shrugged. "I don't care. If you want to."

"Danny's okay," he said. "And he is a good friend. You'll have to give him credit for that, he's loyal. And," he added, giving her a quick glance, "thanks for setting me straight on how you feel about Russ. I wasn't sure."

"I meant it when I said I feel sorry for him. I know he's hurting, and I'm not passing judgment on him. I guess everyone has to handle things his or her own way." Emily sighed. "I'm having enough trouble getting myself straightened out so I know where I'm at. I'm in no position to point a finger at Russ."

Chet took her by the arm. "Come on, let me show you Danny's furniture."

Emily followed Chet around the barn. As he had said, there wasn't much, two end tables that still had to be stained, the small cabinet that Chet was picking up for his father, a tall chest of drawers, and a copy of a Shaker rocking chair. Emily examined the pieces with disbelief. "Did he really make all this by himself?"

"He sure did. You like them?"

"They're beautiful. They're . . ." She didn't say what was in her mind.

"They're what?" Chet asked.

"They just seem so different from Danny." She was embarrassed and fumbling for words. The furniture was so simple and beautiful, it was hard for her to believe they were created by the boy she had been talking to. Yet he had been sensitive to Russ and Russ's problem, so she had no right to think Danny was crude. Emily shook her head impatiently. If she didn't want to be a snob, she had to stop judging people by where they lived or how they dressed. Danny could have more on the ball than all the kids in Hogan's Bridge Farm.

Before they left, Chet opened the door to Danny's

workroom, called in a good-bye, and told him he was taking the cabinet. Danny offered to help, but Chet said he could handle it. Emily stuck her head in the door and said, "Your furniture is beautiful. Thank you for letting me see it."

"Anytime," Danny called back, hardly looking up from the board he was sanding.

Chet carried the cabinet out to the car and put it in the back of the station wagon. On the way home Emily asked how his mother was doing.

"My father's finally convinced her to see a psychiatrist. She needs help, and I hope she gets it."

"Is she feeling any better?"

"I don't know. She's only seen the doctor once so far."

"Should I go to see her?"

"I don't know that, either. Maybe wait a little while until she's seen the shrink a few times. He may be trying to get her to give up Joey's room, and if you come over, she may want to stay there."

"Why don't you let me know when it's okay to see her? I don't want her to think I've just stopped coming over."

"Sure thing." Chet took Emily to her door. She wanted to ask him if he'd like to visit for a while, but she felt shy. So she just thanked him for taking her over to Danny's and went into the house.

She found her mother in the kitchen baking bread. After watching Mrs. Simpson in silence for a few minutes, Emily decided to ask her the question that had been on her mind since Christmas. "Are you still planning to go to Grandma's?" she asked.

"I think so. Just for a few days."

"What about New Year's?" The next day was New Year's Eve.

"What about it? I hate New Year's Eve parties. It may be a good time to go."

"What would Dad think? He wouldn't like that."

"Maybe he'd welcome it. He wouldn't have to drag me around to his parties. Do you want to come?"

"When are you going?"

"Anytime. In fact, we could go this afternoon. Just get in the car and go. I can call Grandma right now. She'll be delighted."

"I'm game," Emily said spontaneously.

The idea grabbed her. To be away for a couple of days, away from everything, seemed a gift from heaven at that moment. Although she had pointed out the facts to Danny, his accusation about Russ had hurt. Perhaps she had been a rotten friend—she had been so involved with her own pain, she had shown little compassion for Russ, and she had certainly been unfair to Danny. What must Chet think of her? "Let's go," she said to her mother. She felt a tremendous urgency to get away, to be someplace where she could get a grip on herself and sort out all the misconceptions. "Go call Grandma. What about Dad? Are you going to call him?" Mr. Simpson had not yet come home from the office.

Emily waited while her mother dialed the phone. It was easy to imagine what her father was saying from her mother's end of the conversation: "Just for a few days. . . . I thought you might welcome it. . . . You can go to all the parties you want tomorrow. . . . I'm not deserting you, please don't say that. Don't get so excited, it's just for a couple of days. I wish you'd understand, I *need* to get away. . . . Yes, Emily's coming with me. . . . Surely I have a right to go and visit my mother. . . . But I don't care about New Year's, I hate New Year's Eve parties. . . . I'm sorry you feel that way. . . . Yes, I'm going to go. Goodbye."

Her mother's eyes were blazing when she hung up the phone. Emily didn't ask any questions. Her mother was clearly angry.

"Okay, let's get ready and go. I'll call Grandma. You don't need to take much," Mrs. Simpson said crisply. She spoke and moved with a determination that was new to Emily.

Less than an hour later, they were in her mother's compact car driving to the highway to get to her mother's house. They had about a three-hour drive, and since they hadn't bothered to have lunch at home, Emily's mother had packed sandwiches and a thermos of hot tea that they could eat on the road. It was a cold but bright sunny day, and Emily felt as if she were leaving all her cares behind her. Maybe just forgetting about everything would be the best way to straighten out her thoughts. Sometimes it worked that way for her.

It was late afternoon and almost dark when they arrived at the farm. Emily's grandmother, Mrs. Heacock, was a widow who lived by herself. Originally, her husband had grown tobacco, but for several years sales began to slack off, and before he died, he had given that up. He left his wife a few cows for milk, some chickens, and a goat. A hired man, Frank, came in to help with the animals.

Mrs. Heacock was a straight-backed, independent woman in her seventies with a mind of her own. Emily felt good the minute she was folded into her grandmother's ample arms. The house was filled with the special smell of home-baked bread and pies mixed with some scented cleanser that was doused around the kitchen. Walking in was like peeling off the outer skins of an onion and getting to the nice, clean, tender part inside.

It was a small, old house, and Emily and her mother shared the guest bedroom upstairs opposite her grandmother's room.

They were all hungry and had an early supper. Emily and her mother cleaned up the dishes, and when they were finished, the three women continued to sit around the kitchen table.

"Now, tell me what brought you here," Mrs. Heacock asked her daughter.

"We came to see you," Mrs. Simpson said with a smile.

"Don't try to fool me. The day before New Year's Eve, all of a sudden you come to visit an old lady. I wasn't born yesterday."

"There honestly wasn't one special thing. I'm not trying to hide anything from you. Steve and I have our disagreements. I guess they're getting worse." Mrs. Simpson looked at her mother wistfully. "I wanted to get away and sort things out."

"I hope you do. Don't be a fool, Vivian. You have a good marriage. Steve is a good man."

"I know that. He's a wonderful man and I love him. But I don't like the way we live."

"You don't like the way *he* lives." Mrs. Heacock

gave her daughter a knowing smile. "You're mixing things up. He has a life with his work, separate from you. What you need is your own life. You're trying to live his life, and that's what you don't like." She sat back in her chair with an air of satisfaction.

"Mama, we are married. We live together, we don't have separate lives." Emily's mother strung out her words patiently.

"That's where you're wrong. Everybody has to have his or her own life. You have one life together and one separate. You think I cared so much about your father's tobacco? For him it was exciting to see the young tobacco leaves—for me it was just a way to make a living. I had my garden; my flowers were more important to me than tobacco. You have to have something of your own, Viv."

"I suppose you're right," Mrs. Simpson said, "but you have to want something badly. You do or you don't."

"Rubbish." Mrs. Heacock shook her head impatiently. "You can cultivate something. You like flowers, why don't you go work in a nursery? Or play the piano. You used to play. I bet you haven't touched a piano in years."

"I gave my piano away," Mrs. Simpson said.

"Then get another. I don't care what you do, but find something that you enjoy and do it. Go back to school if you want to. You're a lucky woman, Vivian. You don't have to earn a living, you can choose to do anything you want. You've been lazy."

"I'm *not* lazy," her daughter said indignantly. "You don't know all the things I do, I have to do."

"I'm not talking about that kind of laziness. I know you market and cook and entertain and do a lot of chores and errands. But you've been lazy about your *own* life, your mind and soul. You have to find a purpose for yourself."

"All right, Mama, you've made your point. I know what you're saying and I take it to heart. I came here to think, and you've given me something to think about and I will."

"Good." She turned to her granddaughter. "You know what I'm talking about, I'm sure. How are you doing, Emily?"

"Not so great. I have to think things out too. Do you mind if I go out for a walk?"

"It's pretty dark out there. Take a flashlight and don't go far," her grandmother cautioned. "You can't, anyway. Our dirt road goes only to the highway, and you don't want to walk there. Tomorrow you can go in the woods, but I don't advise it at night. There are too many different paths and you could get lost."

"I'll just walk along the road a way," Emily said.

The kitchen had begun to feel stuffy and the conversation disturbing.

Outside, Emily breathed in deeply, savoring the fresh crispness in the air, the country smell of the woods; even the musty barn smell seemed good. She picked her way to the dirt road and walked along the side. There were many more stars than she ever saw at home, and a bright moon lit the road better than a flashlight.

She had started out believing she was going to commune with the stars, that alone in the darkness she would have meaningful thoughts, and that out of the mystery of the night answers would be given to her. Instead, she found she had only questions. What had her grandmother meant when she said her mother's life should have a purpose? Not everyone was destined to do great deeds or to change the world. Perhaps one didn't have to. The trouble with her mother—and with Mrs. Bernstein for that matter, too—was that they had nothing they were really interested in or involved with for themselves. Mrs. Bernstein kept mourning Joey because she had nothing else, and Emily's mother drifted from day to day not liking the country-club life of Hogan's Bridge Farm but not doing anything about making a life for herself.

Emily was determined to be different. Going to

school and hanging out with her friends wasn't enough. She suddenly realized how much taking care of Joey had filled a need in her life. It wasn't only earning the money; what had made Emily feel good was the way he and his family had depended on her, the sense of responsibility the job had given her—and how wonderful it had been to watch Joey respond to the games she taught him and the books she read to him. Even as Emily had these thoughts she had to laugh at herself in the dark. Taking care of one little boy was certainly no grand purpose. But she didn't care. Maybe it was insignificant, but it had been important to her, and now she was going to find something else. But what it would be, she didn't know.

Back in the warm kitchen, she found her grandmother and mother still talking. Emily felt sleepy, so she kissed them both good night and went up to bed.

The next day was a quiet one. They ate, walked, and talked, but no one picked up on any of the conversation from the night before. Emily felt that her mother was less tense, and she herself felt that she was ridding her mind of some of its confusion. Wisely, her grandmother didn't offer any more advice and devoted herself to giving them "good, healthy country food." While Emily enjoyed the serenity, by the afternoon she felt restless and was anxious to go home. The day before, she couldn't wait to get away, and now she was eager to leave.

Chet was very much on her mind. She wondered if he was going to any party on New Year's Eve—more likely he would stay home with his parents. That thought was comforting. She kept seeing him and defined a quality in his face, in his eyes, that intrigued her: He looked as if he knew profound truths. But the answer that she wanted most to know eluded her: What did he think of her? He had been open and nice to her, yet she felt that the tragedy of Joey's death stood between them. She didn't believe that he blamed her for it, yet she felt that they were both always aware of it. While there were moments when the fact that he was Joey's brother made her feel closer to him, she couldn't shake the feeling that he held the accident against her.

Emily was glad that her mother said they would leave early the next morning. "We can at least spend part of New Year's Day with Dad," Mrs. Simpson said. Emily didn't dare ask if her mother had made any decisions about what she was going to do.

When they got home around midday, they found Mr. Simpson in old work pants and a work shirt, waxing the living room floor. Emily had been worried about how her parents would greet each other, but she hadn't expected this. Her father's preoccupation with the floor took both her mother and herself by surprise and relieved the tension. Waxing a floor was so down-to-earth, it couldn't be the prelude to a divorce.

Mrs. Simpson eyed her husband in astonishment. "What got into you?" she asked after they had greeted each other.

"Nothing. The floor looked lousy, so I decided to do a job on it. Do you mind?"

"Mind? I should say not, I'm delighted. Is this part of a New Year's resolution?"

Emily's father grinned sheepishly. "Could be. I know you two went off to do some profound thinking. We've all been shaken up by little Joey's death—you're not the only ones. I've been doing some thinking too. And I'm willing to admit I haven't been paying enough attention to my home and my family. A man can get too involved with his work."

Mrs. Simpson's face broke into a smile. She didn't say anything. She went over and gave her husband a gentle kiss on the mouth. Emily had stood by, listening to them. Because she knew how difficult it was for her father to express his feelings, she realized how much his few words meant to her mother. "I guess you two should be alone," she said. She turned to leave the room.

"No, come here." Her father stretched out his arm and pulled her to him and her mother. "I know you've been having a rough time," he said to Emily. "I'm sorry if I let you down. I don't mean to. I get busy and figure your mother can take care of the emotional problems in this family. I'm not much good at that. But I love you both and I'll try. Yes, I'll try, that's all I can say."

"That's a lot," his wife said. "That's all anyone can promise." Her eyes were bright, and Emily thought she might cry, but instead, she broke the emotional tension. "I expected to find you with a hangover," she said teasingly. "Did you have a good time last night?"

"I stayed home. I fixed supper, had a few beers, and was in bed by ten o'clock. I didn't even stay up to watch the New Year in on TV." He looked at her triumphantly. "How do you like that?"

"I thought it was important that you go to those parties."

"I thought it was, too, but I changed my mind. Do you want me to say I didn't want to go without you?"

"I probably wouldn't believe you."

"It's partly true. I don't enjoy going out without you, believe it or not. But I felt like staying home. Now I'm going to finish my waxing, and then we'll have a fancy New Year's meal. A celebration for just the Simpson family."

"Sounds good to me."

Emily was in her room getting ready to take a

shower when she heard her mother exclaiming in the kitchen. She went in to find out what she was excited about. "Look." Her mother had the refrigerator open. "See what your father did." The shelves were stocked with fancy cheeses, smoked fish, fruit, interesting-looking jars of expensive goodies, and two bottles of champagne.

"Wow, we're going to have a feast." Emily kissed her mother. "I guess you were smart to go away."

"No, I was smart to come back. And what about you? How are you?"

"I'm okay, I'm going to be fine."

Emily felt that after she did a couple of things she had decided she had to do, she *would* be fine.

While she was showering and getting dressed, she thought about the past two days and her parents. They were both DHBs—Decent Human Beings. DHB was a private shorthand she and Becky used when talking about people in town, and teachers and students in school. When it came down to it, that was where you had to start. From there you could go anywhere, she decided.

While Emily was rubbing herself dry with her bath towel, she had an inspiration. She was going to do something with children—maybe volunteer in a hospital or find out if she could do something in the Children's Services organization. The idea filled her with a tremendous exhilaration, and she couldn't wait to tell her parents.

At their festive dinner table, when her father made a toast to the New Year, Emily told them what she planned to do. "It would be a way of honoring Joey," she said. "Something to do in his memory."

"That's lovely," Mrs. Simpson said, turning from Emily to her husband, "but you should be doing it for yourself. I don't mean in a selfish way, and to honor Joey is okay, but you don't need a rationale. You do it because you want to do it. Don't you agree?" she asked her husband.

"Yes, I do," he said, meeting her eyes. "As you said, everyone should have a focus in his or her life."

Obviously, Emily realized, her parents had been talking.

"I guess my focus is you, this house, and Emily," her mother said with a laugh. "But I intend to go back to my piano. That's my New Year's resolution. I'm not a social person."

"I'll try to remember that," Mr. Simpson said, and stretched out his hand to give his wife's hand a squeeze.

It was a relief to Emily to be back in school. She was eager to overcome her self-imposed isolation. Although Becky had assured her that it was all in her head, Emily had felt uncomfortable, wondering if the kids in school thought she was responsible for the accident. Spending time with Mrs. Bernstein had been her excuse, but she knew that if she had wanted to, she still could have seen her friends.

At school Emily immediately sought out Becky.

"Hello, stranger," Becky said. "Have you decided to surface?"

"Hi. Can we have lunch together?" Emily asked. "I love your blouse. Was it a Christmas present?"

"Yeah, from my grandmother. I'll meet you in the cafeteria. Twelve-thirty okay?"

Emily consulted her schedule. "Yeah, that's fine. See you."

"Your hair looks pretty," Becky called after her, and Emily knew that meant they were still good friends.

Emily got to the cafeteria a few minutes early. She filled her tray with a bowl of soup and a sandwich and made for an empty table she spotted off in a corner of the room. Becky joined her soon after she had sat down. All morning Emily had been thinking about how she could explain her feelings to Becky, but she was still vague as to what to say.

"I know I've been acting weird," she started off. "I guess I've been going through some kind of a crisis, but I think I'm coming out of it. I hope you haven't given up on me?" She looked at her friend plaintively.

"I was pretty close," Becky admitted. "I thought of you as my best friend, and I thought you felt the same. But the way you kept hanging around with Chet's mother, you seemed so out of it, like you were in another world."

"I guess I was. I've been doing a lot of thinking. I haven't been very nice to Russ, either."

"Are you going to go back with him?" Becky finished her soup and exchanged her empty bowl for her sandwich.

"No, it can't be the same again, although I still want to be friends with Russ," she added quickly. Emily moved anxiously in her chair and adjusted her blouse. "Becky," she said finally, "I've got to tell you something, but I'm afraid you'll laugh at me."

"You know I won't. What is it?"

"I can't stop thinking about Chet, Chet Bernstein. It's wild, I know, but I think about him all the time."

"*Chet Bernstein?*" Becky was surprised, to say the least. "Are you crazy?"

"I know how incredible it seems, because of Joey. And I don't know really how he feels, except I don't think he hates me. In fact, I keep getting the idea that he may like me a little. The thing is, we both loved

Joey, and instead of the accident keeping us apart, it should bring us together, don't you think?"

Becky looked dubious. "But you were in the car," she said gently. "I know it wasn't your fault—nor Russ's, either. I mean, there was the fog and Joey had that mask on and all, but still . . ."

"Still *what?*" Emily looked directly into Becky's eyes and held them. "Listen, I've been living with this thing until I think I'm going nuts, but I'm coming out of it now. I've gone over it in my head a million times, and I know that there was nothing in the world I could have done. My being in the car had nothing to do with it—if I hadn't been and Joey had run out the same way, it would have happened exactly the same. I don't think it's helped anyone to lay the blame on someone—not on Russ, either. Golly, if Mrs. Bernstein can forgive me, forgive Russ, I should think everyone else could too. It was an accident, period."

Becky looked mollified. "I wasn't trying to blame you. You're the one who's been feeling guilty."

"I know, I'm sorry if I sounded like I was blowing my top. I'm sick of feeling guilty and thinking everyone is looking at me strangely. I have to live with myself and get straight about it. I really loved Joey and it was a horrible tragedy, but it shouldn't destroy

Russ or me." She glanced at Becky shyly. "I'm going to find some work to do with little kids. I like them, and maybe I can help at the hospital for handicapped children or with the Children's Services."

"That's terrific." Becky gave Emily a hug. "You're gonna be okay. I'm glad."

"I'd like to do something about Russ. He's been having a rough time."

Becky looked a little surprised. "I thought you were finished with him."

"I don't want him for a boyfriend. But I've come down hard on him, criticizing him instead of realizing he was hurting the same as I was. It hit us in different ways."

"What are you thinking of doing?" Becky was skeptical but intrigued.

"Well . . ." Emily was hesitant. "You know he's a friend of Danny's, and now it turns out Chet is a friend of Danny's too. I thought of doing something wild, like asking the three of them over . . . Don't laugh. Chet sounded a little like he felt sorry for Russ, and maybe if they met face-to-face, they would stop hating each other. It's worth a try."

"You are really crazy. They'll kill each other. Remember what happened at the pub."

"I know. But this'll be different. Danny's friends with both of them. I don't expect them to be buddy-

buddy, but I think that if they were at my house, they'd be okay. All I want is for Chet to stop blaming Russ, and for Russ to stop blaming himself. They don't have to kiss and make up, but if they just understand where the other's at, they'll probably both feel better. I'm doing this for Joey, if you want the truth—I hate for them to be hurting and mad at each other for no reason on account of him. It doesn't seem right."

"I wish you luck," Becky said.

"Say, would you come over too? Of course I've got to get them to come, but if you were there, too, it would help."

Becky looked dubious. "I don't know what good I'd do. But I'll come." Her face brightened. "Sure, I wouldn't miss it for anything. Who knows what may happen?"

That afternoon, after school, Emily tried to get up her courage to call the three boys to set up a date for them to come over. But first she decided that she had to see Mrs. Bernstein. She wanted the reassurance that they were still friends, and she wanted to talk to her.

Determinedly, she went over to the Bernstein house and rang the bell. Mrs. Bernstein opened the door and seemed pleased to see her.

"Come in. I'm so glad to see you. Where have you been?" Mrs. Bernstein kissed her warmly. "I thought you'd forgotten all about me."

"I'd never do that. How are you?" Emily thought she seemed nervous and strained.

"I'm all right, I guess. I've been seeing a doctor and taking pills to sleep." She sat down nervously and motioned to Emily to join her on the sofa. "My husband and Chet have been cleaning out Joey's room. They want to make it into some kind of a den, but I don't know what we need a den for. I'm not supposed to go up there and sit, but since you're here and I haven't been in the room for days, do you think we could go up for a little while?" She turned to Emily pleadingly.

"No, I don't think so," Emily said gently but firmly. "I've been thinking about things, Mrs. Bernstein, and I don't think it was good for us to spend all that time in Joey's room."

Mrs. Bernstein looked wounded. "You sound like all the others," she said, giving Emily a disappointed look. "I thought you understood and that you loved Joey too."

"I did love Joey, very much. That's why I think you can't go on mourning forever. Joey was so alive—thinking about him made me think we have to celebrate being alive. I never thought about life and death before this happened. But everything dies. Flowers, animals, people—if everybody sat around feeling sorry for themselves because something or someone died, the world would be a terrible place. I mean, since you know that someday you are going to die, too, it's stupid not to make the most of being alive. That's what I intend to do, and you should do the same. You've got so much—your house, Chet, your husband—it would be awful to waste it."

Mrs. Bernstein had been sitting still and listening quietly. She laughed softly. "I don't know why I'm spending so much money going to a doctor. You're saying pretty much the same things he says. You're a smart girl, Emily."

"I'm not that smart," Emily said emphatically. "It's taken me a long time to figure things out. It seems so clear once you think things out."

"I'm trying hard, Emily, I really am. I'm working at it. Would you like to go out? Come on, I'll buy you some ice cream or a soda. Whatever you'd like."

"That would be nice."

Outside, Mrs. Bernstein tucked her arm under Emily's. "Did my husband put you up to coming to talk to me?" she asked.

"Absolutely not. No one put me up to it. I came

because I wanted to see you, and I felt I hadn't done the right thing before. I'm not sorry, but I wanted to straighten things out."

"I'm glad that you did."

Sitting in the coffee shop, they didn't talk about Joey. Mrs. Bernstein asked Emily about school, and they talked about the village and people they both knew. Emily felt that Joey's mother was making an effort to be natural and at ease, but she could tell it was a strain. She was sure that they were both relieved when they were finished and could go home.

Emily walked Mrs. Bernstein to her door and met Chet, who was just returning home too. He was surprised to see them together. "Where have you two been?"

"Out having sodas," his mother said. "Emily came to visit me." She gave Emily an affectionate look.

"That was nice."

"I've got to go now," Emily said. "I'll see you soon."

She turned to leave them but found Chet walking alongside her. "I'll walk you home."

They fell into step together. "How'd you find my mom?" he asked.

"She seemed great. Much better. I guess her doctor's helping her. I'm glad I went to see her—I hope you and your father don't mind."

"No, of course not. We just worried about her sitting up in Joey's room. But she's not doing that anymore."

"I know."

While they were walking, Emily was trying to get up her courage to ask Chet to come over. She felt shy, though, because he still seemed somewhat remote. Not stuck-up, she decided, but into himself, as if he were in the process of solving some cosmic problem. "What are you doing Friday night?" she asked finally.

Chet caught her eyes and held them. "Nothing in particular. Why?"

"I thought if you had nothing better to do, you'd come over and bring Danny. I'd like him to know I made a mistake about him."

"I can ask him. I don't know if he'll come."

"I know, but I hope he will."

They didn't say anything more about Friday night, and when Emily left him at her house, she wasn't sure if he would turn up or not and, if he did, whether Danny would be with him. She was annoyed with herself for not pinning him down, but she also knew that she couldn't have. The big question now was whether or not to ask Russ.

When she discussed the situation with Becky, her friend said absolutely to ask him. "The worst that can happen is that only Russ and I will be there. That's not so bad. Besides, wasn't that the whole point, to get Chet and Russ together?"

"If Russ will even come," Emily said dolefully. She was beginning to wonder why she had started the whole thing. What would she say if Russ, Chet, and Danny all showed up? Who did she think she was, trying to get people to talk things out and try to understand each other better?

When she told her parents later that evening that she had asked the three boys and Becky over for Friday night, her father asked the same question. "What are you trying to do, honey? Are you planning to run a peace conference?" He laughed. "My daughter the diplomat. They could use you at the UN. I wish you luck."

"I think it's very noble of Emily. Those boys shouldn't be fighting with each other. It's ridiculous. I approve." Her mother nodded to her.

"I'm not disapproving," Mr. Simpson said. "I admire her, I only hope it works."

All day Friday, Emily was nervous, thinking about the evening. Russ had been surprised when she'd called him, and he had asked what was up. "Nothing special," Emily had told him. "Becky's coming over and maybe a couple of other kids. No party. We haven't seen each other for a long time."

"Not my fault," he'd said curtly. "Okay, I'll come by around eight, okay?"

"That'll be great."

At school she saw Chet only from a distance, and she wasn't sure if he'd show up with Danny. But she decided to be prepared. After classes, Becky came over and they bought pizza dough and sodas, and made pizzas in the Simpsons' kitchen.

"What are you going to say to the guys when they get here?" Becky wanted to know.

"I have no idea. Maybe I won't say anything. I just hope they don't get into a fight. Maybe they won't come," she said hopefully. "You and I can eat all the pizzas."

"No thank you. They'll come, why shouldn't they?"

"I don't know. Just wishful thinking."

Emily could barely eat any supper. "I'll eat later," she told her parents.

"Nothing terrible is going to happen," her mother assured her, aware of Emily's anxiety. "What you are doing is very nice, and either it will work or it won't. But there's nothing for you to be anxious about."

"Except making a fool of myself, that's all. I may end up with no one talking to me."

"I don't think that will happen," her mother said.

Emily was grateful to her parents for taking off to the movies, although, when she kissed them good-bye, she felt that her last friends in the world, except Becky, were leaving her.

Becky came over before eight, and as it drew close to the time for someone to arrive, Emily became more and more nervous. "Don't be so jumpy," Becky said, then jumped when the Simpsons' hall clock boomed out the hour.

"I can't help it." Emily was nervously walking around the living room, plumping up pillows, moving a chair a few inches one way and then another.

Both girls jumped again when the door bell rang. "I'll get it." Becky made for the hall.

Russ came into the room with her. "Hi," he greeted Emily. He glanced around the room. "Where's everybody?"

"No one's here yet," Emily said. "I told you it wasn't a party. Just a couple of kids coming over. I have a new tape I'll put on."

Emily slipped in the tape and sat down on a hassock. Becky was sprawled on a sofa, and Russ fidgeted around the room. He seemed decidedly uncomfortable. They all listened, saying nothing until the music ended. Finally Russ swung around to Emily. "What's going on? I have a funny feeling that you asked me over for a reason. What's on your little mind?"

Emily gave a nervous laugh. "My mind's not so little."

"Devious, then. Something's going on. You two are acting like you've got some big secret. Let me in on it."

"There is no secret." Just then the door bell rang and Becky jumped up. "I'll get it."

Emily felt her heart beginning to thump, and her stomach felt uneasy. She was hoping desperately that it wasn't Chet and Danny. But in a minute they were in the room with Becky behind them. Russ stared at the two boys, and they stared at him.

Russ broke the silence in the room. "I knew she was up to something. I don't know what's on your mind, Emily, but I'm getting out of here. I think you've gone nuts."

"No, I haven't." Emily's voice was stronger than she felt. "Please don't go. I'm not up to anything, and I'm not being devious. I just thought that since Danny was your friend, Russ, and also a friend of Chet's, it was stupid for you and Chet to be mad at each other."

Danny laughed. "What am I, some kind of a go-between?"

"Maybe. Anyway, you're all here, so I'll put on some more music. Becky and I made pizzas and we've got a pile of sodas."

"I'll get the stuff from the kitchen," Becky offered.

Emily kept watching Russ while she put on another tape. He was standing at the door, as if undecided what he wanted to do. Then Becky called him into the kitchen to help her carry the food and drinks in. Chet had stood by quietly watching the others, as if he were trying to figure out what was going on.

"Well, here we are." Emily tried to sound gay while she made room on a table for the trays Becky and Russ brought in. "Come on, guys, dig in."

Danny was the only one who seemed relaxed. He helped himself to a large slice of pizza and took a soda. "I don't know what's going on," he said, making himself comfortable on the sofa, "but the food's good."

"Nothing's going on." Becky brought over her plate and sat next to him.

Emily looked from Russ to Chet. "Well, let's eat." Russ sat on one chair and Chet on another, and Emily sat on a hassock facing everyone. "You look as if you're holding a meeting," Chet remarked.

Emily felt that the tension in the room was too much. She couldn't stand it anymore. "Okay, so I did ask you over for a reason. But it's no big deal. It's no more than I said before. I think it's awful that we can't all be friends. I'm willing to admit that I acted dumb toward Russ, and I put Danny down, and I was wrong. I guess that's the main thing I want to say, that I made a mistake and I'm sorry. I'm not trying to be a peacemaker or a do-gooder, but Joey's death has made me think about a lot of things. That was senseless, and I can't stand people hating each other because of it. That's just as senseless."

Emily picked up a can of soda and drank from it thirstily. She was afraid to look at anyone, but when she did, everyone looked serious except Danny. He had a small smile on his face.

"You sound like my dad when he carries on about being out of a job," he said. "He gets mad at everyone, and then he says, 'What's the use of being mad? That's not going to do any good.'" Danny looked around from one face to another. "I don't understand you guys. You've got it made, you have everything, so you invent problems for yourself. Wise up. I'm gonna put on some music." He picked out a tape from Emily's collection and put it on to play. In a few minutes he was dancing by himself around the room. He was a good dancer, and Becky jumped up and joined him. Emily, Chet, and Russ sat watching them. It was an uneasy silence.

"Aren't you two going to say anything?" Emily finally demanded.

"What's there to say?" Russ asked.

"I don't know. I thought . . ." She didn't finish her sentence.

"What did you think?" Chet asked. "That Russ and I were going to kiss and say that we loved each other? That's not going to happen. I'll be honest with you. I don't think I'll ever be able to look at Russ without thinking about him driving the car that killed my kid brother. But I know that's strictly an emotional reaction. My head tells me that it probably wasn't his fault, that he's hurting because of it and I shouldn't hold it against him. But I'll never be buddy-buddy. You understand what I'm saying?"

"I guess I do," Emily said in a low voice. She turned to Russ. "I guess I was a dope to invite you two over."

"No, it's okay. I know how he feels, and I guess he can't help it. Maybe we understand each other better now and we don't have to knock each other around anymore." He stood up. "I'm taking off. Thanks for the pizza. Danny, I've got to go."

"Go ahead, I'm sticking around for a while. See you."

Emily walked Russ to the door. "You're not mad at me for asking you and Chet over, are you?" She realized he was never going to talk about how he felt, and she had to respect that.

"No, and I'm glad you got squared away with Danny. He's a nice guy. You think I didn't really care about what happened to Joey, but I do, and I'm still working my way out of it. Danny's been a good friend." Clearly Russ had been badly hurt by what had happened, and Emily felt he *would* work it out in his own way.

"I know, and I hope we can be friends again too."

"Sure, why not?" He bent down and gave her a light kiss on the cheek. "Go back to your company." He glanced into the room where Becky and Danny were whirling around the room as if they'd danced together for years. "They're having a good time," Russ said. "Funny if they ended up a couple."

"You never can tell."

With Russ gone, Emily went back to the others. Chet had picked up a magazine and was reading it.

"You don't like to dance?" she asked.

"I don't mind. You want to?"

To Emily's surprise, Chet turned out to be a fantastic dancer. He had perfect rhythm and danced with his whole body. At first, she had trouble keeping up with him, but she was quick and graceful, and soon they were dancing as well and as frantically as Becky and Danny. When the tape came to an end the four of them sat down breathlessly.

But in a few minutes Danny jumped up and put on another tape. For the next couple of hours the two couples danced, stopping only long enough to change the music. It was after ten o'clock when Becky sank down on the sofa, protesting that she was exhausted.

"Come on, I'll take you home," Danny said to Becky. "You don't need a ride home, do you?" he asked Chet.

"No, I'm just a few blocks away. I can walk."

Becky followed Danny out the door, after promising Emily she'd call her the next day.

Alone with Chet, Emily put another tape on to play, but Chet didn't get up to dance. "Come and sit down," he said, motioning to the place beside him on the sofa. "Do you think your party was a success?" He had his arm behind her along the back of the sofa.

"It wasn't a party. But I'm not sorry I asked all of you over. Some important things were said, and I know I feel better."

Having Chet sit that close to her filled Emily with a yearning she wasn't sure she could handle. She kept wanting to turn around and put her arms around him. She felt that in his arms, she would at last find the comfort she had been seeking since the accident. If he held her close, her pain would flow from her. But that would never happen. Chet probably liked her as little as he did Russ. After all, she, too, was in the car that had killed his brother.

Chet's arm slid down, and his hand touched her shoulder. She couldn't bear it any longer. The weeks of pain and sorrow and guilt overflowed inside her.

Emily turned and buried her face against his shirt. She couldn't hold back her sobs. Chet put his arms around her and held her close to him.

"I'm sorry," she mumbled. "I don't know what brought this on. . . ."

"Don't worry, go ahead and cry." He stroked her hair gently. "There's nothing wrong with crying."

She felt she had been sobbing for hours, although she knew it was only minutes later that she pulled up her head. "I'm sorry . . . for everything. . . ."

"Don't be sorry," Chet said, and handed her a handkerchief. He held her face in his hands. "You mustn't be sorry. I'm the one to be sorry. I've been fighting with *myself*. Every time I've been with you I wanted to touch you, hold you . . . it used to drive me nuts when my mother talked about how terrific you were, as if I didn't know. But then I kept thinking of Joey and the funeral and imagining you and Russ in the car, laughing and talking to each other, and I'd make myself freeze up."

Emily pulled away from him and covered her face with her hands. "I don't blame you for hating me."

He pulled her hands away. "You little dope. Don't you see? I don't hate you. I love you. Don't you understand? I was fighting because I was falling for you, and it seemed too unreal. But I know . . . I knew all the time that it wasn't your fault. Some part of me knew, anyway. Part of it was being jealous of Russ—I wanted to hate both of you, so he got the brunt of it. But it's all getting washed out. I don't want to hate Russ, and I love you. . . ."

Emily's eyes were still filled with tears. She gave a deep sigh. "I'm sure glad I asked you over here tonight," she said, and nestled in his arms.